THEY ALL HAD A REASON

A rumor. A secret. A lie. A murder.
(They All Had A Reason. Book 1)

Michele Leathers

EMAR Publishing

Cover design by: Marissa Lete
Library of Congress Control Number: 2018675309
Printed in the United States of America

To Ryan

CHAPTER 1

I remain silent, nearly motionless, with each deliberate shallow breath. I'm focused intently on the muffled conversation happening only a few feet away. The darkness around me is barely penetrated by a thin beam of light coming from the other side of the closet door. My mind is processing the shocking secret I have just overheard. It's not one of those secrets I am bound to keep out of loyalty, nor is it a secret I plan to use as blackmail. But I am most definitely going to expose it tonight, because the person it involves deserves to know the truth. And if I am being completely honest, there is also a small matter of revenge that is long overdue.

Some time after the room falls silent, I abandon my hiding place in the closet and enter the bedroom again, where I'm surrounded by innumerable selfies plastered all over the walls: exaggerated smiling, pouty duck lips, tongue sticking out, trying way too hard to appear indifferent, all the usual stuff. These are interspersed with thirteen mirrors of various shapes and sizes. I realize that's an oddly specific fact. I just couldn't help but count them. Who decorates a room like this? A narcissist? Someone suffering from delusions of grandeur? In my opinion, both these diagnoses would be correct, since I know the person in every one of these pictures. It's Bellany Silverfield, the girl who is ruining my life.

I slowly push the bedroom door open a couple inches. Thumping bass pumps down the hallway, mingled with random laughter and imperceptible conversations. I take a quick visual survey of the people hovering close by. Once I feel confident that

Bellany is nowhere around, I slip back into the crowded hallway, hoping nobody notices what room I just came out of.

"Hey, Charlotte," a deep male voice calls moments later. I turn to see who it is without making direct eye contact, trying to appear as if I hadn't heard him. He is unconvinced, taking a step into my path and tilting his head to ensure our eyes will meet. It's Damion Johnson, otherwise known as Ace. He's definitely cute, some girls call him hot. He has the face of an angel, but nothing else about him is remotely angelic.

I immediately scan to see where his phone is. It has been strategically placed in the front pocket of his shirt, camera side up. He better not be recording me for his Youtube channel. Most of his videos are random and kind of lame, but occasionally he catches people in scandalous or embarrassing situations, which is why he has thousands of followers. "Hey . . . Ace," I reply, trying not to stare at the camera.

He lifts his chin, signaling in the direction behind me. "Do you know where Bridger's bedroom is?"

"It's two doors down on the left," I say, pointing.

"Thanks." Ace struts past me, pants sagging, plaid boxer shorts exposed, and quickly disappears into Bridger's bedroom.

Now that I'm no longer in danger of being featured in one of his spy videos, my thoughts quickly shift back to that small matter of revenge. I start searching the crowd, looking for Quentin Colson. Some of the people here tonight are strangers, but I recognize a lot of them from school. Most are juniors or seniors at Smithfield-Selma High School. A few are sophomores like me. Quentin should be easy to find. He's a senior, starting forward on the basketball team, super popular, usually the center of attention at parties.

As I round the corner towards the dining room, I find my good friend, Bridger Silverfield. He's the twin brother of the narcissist, Bellany. His dark, shoulder length hair is hanging in his eyes. He looks a little worn down and tired tonight. The Silverfield's housekeeper quit a few weeks ago, and Bridger's father still hasn't hired her replacement. So Bridger skipped school today and stayed home to clean since nobody else in his family ever does. But it's only him, his sister, and his dad. Who would've thought the three of them could be such slobs?

"Are you okay?" I ask him.

Bridger nudges his foot against an overflowing laundry basket sitting underneath the antique mahogany dining room table. "I forgot about this one," he groans, then gives me a helpless look, which I know all too well. "Can you take this down to the laundry room for me?" he asks. "I would do it myself, but I've got to empty the trash can. It's already full, and everybody's throwing their cans and cups on the floor."

I seriously wish he would just ask his sister to take care of this. My eyes scan over the laundry basket. It's full of pastel colors, lots of purples and pinks, so I know they're Bellany's clothes. But whatever. I guess I can put off my search for Quentin, at least for a few more minutes. "Sure." I shrug.

I wonder if Bridger realizes how lucky he is to have *me* for a friend. Not many people would come early to a party to help clean, like I did tonight. Bridger and I spent a couple hours folding laundry, while Bellany was in the bathroom curling her hair and doing her makeup. Yeah, I'm still bitter about it.

Bridger gives his head a flick, tossing his hair out of his downcast eyes. "If this place gets trashed, my dad is going to kill me. He thinks we're only having a couple people over tonight."

The Silverfield's house is a beautifully restored, hundred-year-old Victorian, located a few miles away from historic downtown Smithfield, North Carolina. Choosing to throw a party in a home furnished with expensive and rare antiques wasn't the smartest decision. Luckily, I convinced Bridger to roll up all the handwoven rugs and stash them away in the garage. Those things would have been impossible to clean. The orange and purple Halloween streamers we hung up earlier have already been ripped down, only fragments remain dangling from the ceiling. And people have been playing around with the fake cobwebs that used to be strategically spread over lamps and other furniture. One boy has a cobweb stretched out over his head and face, wearing it like a mask.

"Bridger, if people start getting out of hand, just kick them out. Or end the party." Everybody arrived earlier than they were supposed to, right when Bridger and I were in the middle of putting away laundry. In my opinion, they have been here long enough.

He lets out a heavy exhale, tipping his head back, probably rolling his eyes at me. "I'm not going to make people leave. The chances of mine and my sister's seventeenth birthday landing on the same weekend our dad is out of town are like a million to one. Nobody else's party is ever going to come close to how epic this party is . . ."

I'm only half listening as he continues to justify why it's perfectly fine to go behind his father's back and turn their beautiful family home into a frat house. But maybe I shouldn't be frustrated with Bridger for roping me into helping him clean and decorate this place. After all, if it hadn't been for that, I wouldn't have found out what Bellany is up to. She had no idea I was in her closet putting away a stack of her skinny jeans, when I overheard her juicy phone conversation.

I look down at the laundry basket stuffed under the table that Bridger has obviously tried to hide from his party guests. The sound of glass shattering fills the air. We both turn and look. Then Bridger takes off in hot pursuit, cursing under his breath. I doubt that will be the last thing broken here tonight.

Before I leave the dining room, I take a quick look around in search of Quentin again. But I still don't see him. I pick up the basket, which is a lot heavier than I expect, and start maneuvering through the crowd until I reach the end of the hall. A girl I don't know is standing in front of the basement door, eyes glued to her phone. "Excuse me," I say. "Can you open the door for me?"

"Yeah." She pulls the door open and peers inside. "What's down there?"

I press my shoulder against the light switch on the wall, and the rickety wooden staircase comes into view. Only one side has a railing to hold onto. "The laundry room," I tell her as I step down into an invisible cloud of mildew.

"That looks super spooky," she says. "It kind of reminds me of that scary movie where they clap their hands to make the lights go out, and the girl gets trapped down in the basement--"

"Thanks for opening the door," I cut her off. I know the scary movie she's talking about. I've seen it before. And yes, this basement does look exactly like the one in the movie. Only she didn't need to point that out. I look over my shoulder at her. "Don't close the door. I'm coming right back."

"Uh huh," she mumbles, her attention drawn to her phone again as she walks off.

I'm unable to see the steps in front of me with this huge basket in the way, so I move slowly down the staircase. My plan is to leave Bellany's dirty clothes on the floor next to the open door which leads to the laundry room. I refuse to go any further than that. No need to risk a real life scary movie scenario actually playing out -- not that I really think it would. But just in case.

About midway down the stairs, a sudden vibration rises under my feet, sending a jolt of adrenaline through me. I envision a ghostly demon from the underworld about to attack me from behind. I spin around, almost losing my balance, ready to scream, fight, whatever. Only it's not a demon coming to get me. But it's close. It's Bellany. She's heading down the stairs, wearing painted on skinny jeans and a tight yellow shirt, buttons about to burst. Caramel-colored spiral curls cascade down her shoulders, bouncing with each step she takes.

There have been several instances where someone has mistaken me for being Bellany, but only when they see me from the back. Bellany and I have the same hair color and we both keep it long, almost to our waist. The first time Bellany witnessed someone mistake me for her, she took it as a huge insult. I took it as a compliment.

"Charlotte!" she snaps.

My shoulders cinch up toward my ears at the sound of her

shrill voice. Okay, so she's not here to help with the laundry. I guess I should have noticed the scowl on her face sooner, but I was trying to balance this basket and not drop it or fall down the stairs. Bellany looks like she's about ten notches above angry, nearing the psycho threshold level. If I had to take a guess, I'd say that right now she wants to kick me in my teeth, which she could easily do since she's standing a couple of steps above me, and she has a wicked high kick. I've seen it many times before when she's cheering during pep rallies. Normally, we meet eye to eye. We're both five foot six. But I feel kind of vulnerable here.

She inhales sharply. "Why were you in my bedroom? My friends saw you leave right after I did."

Great. I was afraid she might find out. But I only went into her bedroom to put away a stack of folded clothes, because Bridger asked me to. I didn't intentionally go in there to spy on her or to snoop around. She came in unexpectedly and was talking on her phone, so I figured I would just hide in the closet until she left, because I knew she would get the wrong idea.

I heard her talking on the phone to some guy, and it was obvious they were more than friends. At first, I thought she was talking to her boyfriend, Quentin. But she called this person "big G," which is not her pet name for Quentin. I immediately realized she must be cheating, and I saw this bombshell of a revelation as a perfect opportunity to finally get back at her for the years of havoc she has put me through.

As soon as I find Quentin tonight, I'm going to tell him.

Bellany grabs hold of the other side of the laundry basket and leans in close, her blue eyes cold as ice. "What were you doing in my room, *burger belly*?"

Heat rises in my cheeks. She started calling me this new nickname last week. A few people have asked me what "burger belly" means, then they follow up by saying, "Your stomach isn't fat." It's not Bellany's intention to reference my stomach being fat. She's making fun of the burn scars I have on my stomach. I got them when I was a toddler. Bellany saw my scars this past summer, when she walked in on me while I was changing into my swimsuit.

She gives the laundry basket a slight jostle, fuchsia lips twisting to the right. "Were you looking for more gossip to tell my dad, burger belly?"

I accidentally mentioned in front of her dad last week, that Quentin's mom has a criminal record. When Mr. Silverfield heard this, he about had a stroke. "What crime, or crimes, did she commit?" he asked me. And I couldn't lie to him. I knew he could look it up and find out for himself, anyway. So I told him the truth. I said, "She murdered her husband about fifteen years ago and just got out of prison last year."

I didn't let this information slip out on purpose. I would never do anything intentionally to cause trouble for Quentin. But, the damage had been done, and I couldn't take it back.

To my relief, Quentin forgave me. But I doubt Bellany will ever get over it, because Mr. Silverfield has forbidden her from seeing Quentin. Now she has to sneak around to see him behind her dad's back. Still, regardless of my part in *her* problem, hearing her call me "burger belly" just now has really ticked me off. Her level of cruelty knows no boundaries.

I inhale sharply. "I don't have anything to tell your dad, but I am going to tell Quentin that you're cheating on him. Who's big G?"

"What?" she asks, feigning confusion.

"You know what I'm talking about. Don't play dumb. I recorded your conversation." And that's the truth. I really did record it.

The beautiful face staring back at me -- the straight nose, high cheekbones, sculpted eyebrows -- freezes in place as she processes what I have just told her. What is she going to do, I wonder. Will she beg me not to share the recording with Quentin? Will she try to strike up some kind of a deal with me in exchange for my silence? Will she throw a tantrum? This has got to be the first time I have ever seen Bellany speechless. Defeated. I wish I could take a picture of this rare sight -- it's so much more momentous than seeing Bigfoot or the Loch Ness Monster. This is awesome!

Suddenly a strange look enters her eyes -- not fear or panic. I'm unsure what it is, but it happens so quickly, I don't have time to react. Her fingers release the laundry basket, clothes fly, and so do I. A shock wave of pain surges through my tailbone and back. I strain to keep my head forward, until finally gravity relinquishes its hold, and I'm lying flat on the ground at the bottom of the staircase.

Bellany laughs, mockingly. "You should really be more careful. People have been known to die from falling down stairs." She bends down to pick something up. It's a phone in a black case. Wait! That's my phone! I must have dropped it when I fell. A devious smile spreads across her face. "Looks like you don't have any proof after all."

No! I try to spring to my feet, but I can't move as fast as I want to with a numb tailbone and an aching back. The door at the bottom of the staircase slams shut in my face. I grab hold of the doorknob. It won't budge. "Bellany!" I yell. "Bellany, open the door!"

"Have fun at the party!" She calls from the other side. Footsteps race back up the stairs. The other door slams.

"Bellany!" I pound my fists against the door's hard surface. "Bellany! Somebody!"

I slam my body against the door and kick it over and over again until my foot aches. Frantically, I scan my surroundings. This place is like a prison with its cinder block walls and cement floor. There's a washer, dryer, hot water heater and endless stacks of boxes and storage bins. There's no computer, no phone, no windows. No way out!

I've got to break down this door somehow!

After going through several of the boxes, I find a nail and a toothpick, which I use to try to pick the lock. But it doesn't work.

I pound my fists on the door again and yell as loud as I can. . . .

Nobody comes to help.

I feel like I'm about to start bawling my eyes out. My rate

of breathing is quick, and I can't calm down. I have never felt claustrophobic before, until now. How am I going to get out of here?

I grab a broom and slam the handle up against the ceiling repeatedly. "Can anybody hear me?" I yell. "I'm trapped in the basement! Somebody help me. . . ."

It doesn't take long before my throat begins to ache from yelling and my shoulder strength gives out. I toss the broom on the floor. This is useless. The music up there is blaring and everybody's so loud. They're never going to hear me.

How long am I going to be down here? All night? I can't endure that. It's freezing. There aren't any blankets, just these dirty clothes. There's nowhere comfortable to sit or lay down, and my back is aching.

How does Bellany always get what she wants? She seems to hold some kind of power over the universe to make everything swing her way: She gets the boys she wants, the friends, respect from teachers. I don't understand how she does it. And that's not the only thing that baffles me. I never understood why she hates me so much.

From the moment we first met in middle school, I sensed the contempt she had for me. It was as clear as the sky on a sunny day. When she started stealing my friends, one by one, and then ostracized me from the group, I knew without a doubt she had it out for me. I was, and still am, the target of her evil designs. So I try often, but mostly fail, to beat her in this unofficial quest she has to ruin my life.

Crazy as it may seem, though, there was a time when I had a sliver of hope that we could move past this animosity between us. It happened last year, when Mom started dating Bellany and Bridger's dad. I thought Bellany could learn to like me -- for her dad's sake -- since he and Mom seemed so happy together.

But I learned real quick this dream I had of a combined and happy family was not grounded in reality. Bellany managed to break up our parents' relationship in a matter of months. I'm still mad at myself for getting my hopes up. How delusional was

I to think that she might actually stop hating me or that she would accept Mom?

Bellany was always rude and mean to Mom. She played pranks on her. Stupid, irritating, childish pranks. Like loosening the top of the salt shaker, so that when Mom poured the salt, the entire contents of the container spilled out onto her food.

One time, Bellany dumped a bunch of vinegar and red food coloring into Mom's drink. This was done in conjunction with putting some kind of extreme hot sauce in Mom's bowl of chili. When Mom took a bite of chili, her mouth was on fire. She grabbed her drink and chugged it down. The sour vinegar taste made her gag. She spit the drink out, coughing and choking. Red punch went all over Mom's white outfit and Mr. Silverfield's expensive, hand-woven rug. The stain never came out of the outfit or the rug. When Mom explained to Mr. Silverfield that someone had tampered with her drink and her food, he brushed it off as if it wasn't a big deal. I'm not sure if he even believed Mom. So she told him to take a bite of her chili to see for himself, but he didn't because the chili was inedible, full of red vinegar water.

I think the last straw for Mom that prompted their breakup was when Mr. Silverfield was hosting a fundraiser for a friend's political campaign here at his house. A lot of important and high-end society types were in attendance. Mom was all dressed up and looked beautiful. The party was professionally catered, a string quartet was hired to play music. The swimming pool had a fountain in it, lit up with green lights. Large flowers floated in the water. Mom was wearing high heels and a long, form-fitting dress. She walked by Bellany with a drink in her hand and was distracted, talking to someone. Mom was entirely unprepared for what would happen next. I still can't believe it myself. The whole thing was so ruthless.

Bellany stuck out her foot and intentionally tripped Mom, making her fall straight into the pool. Mom's formal gown quickly became see-through in water. Not only was she humiliated, but her dress was ruined. She had spent over a hundred dollars on that dress -- money she didn't have to spare. Mom's makeup and hair had been professionally done. That also got ruined. When Mom told Mr. Silverfield what Bellany had done, he didn't believe that his daughter would ever intentionally trip Mom. He defended Bellany and said it must have been an accident. But it wasn't an accident.

Bridger was really sad when he found out that our parents had ended their relationship. A couple days later, I went with him to his oral surgery appointment. That was probably the only time I have ever heard him bad-mouth his sister. He said that he felt like Bellany was responsible for their parents' divorce. He said Bellany would always argue with their mom and place their dad in the middle. Whenever their dad wasn't around to hear, she would call their mom fat or ugly to her face. Bellany would tell her mom not to come to her cheer competitions or dance recitals, because she was too embarrassed to be seen with her. Bellany drove their mom to have a nervous breakdown. After their mom got out of a mental institution, she never came back home. Their parents got a divorce.

If Bridger had told me all of this crazy stuff ahead of time, I would never have let Mom date their dad. But I believe Bridger only told me these deep family secrets, because he was doped up after just having had his wisdom teeth removed.

The next day when he was fully lucid, I mentioned the conversation to him, and he denied ever saying those things. He got upset, like seriously mad and called me a liar. I'm sorry, but ruining our friendship over something like that . . . for me, it just wasn't worth it. So I shut up and dropped the subject. I've still never told anyone, well, except for Mom.

I try to push those unpleasant memories aside since they're only making me more upset. I look around at the cinder block walls again. For some reason they feel like they're closing in on me.

If I don't come home tonight, will Mom even notice I'm gone? Will she worry and try to find me? Or will she assume I'm spending the night at my best friend, Gemma

Hernandez's house, like I usually do on weekends? And what about tomorrow? How late will it be before she realizes I'm still missing?

Somehow, I have to get out of here.

I continue going through boxes and bins, looking for *I don't know what*. Maybe I'll find an ax or a saw. Wouldn't that be nice.

After digging for what seems like hours, I find Christmas decorations, old board games, clothes, kitchen items, and ancient toys. Not helpful. I open up another box and find wires, keyboards, and other odds and ends, but there's nothing I can use to break out of here. As I dig further down, I find a flashlight and set it aside. Just in case I need it later.

I head to another stack of boxes and remove the top one, setting it on the ground. I'm about to open the lid when something catches my eye. My mouth falls open, heart skips a beat. There's a small hole in the wall, big enough for me to crawl through. Spider webs dangle in front of it like curtains. I can't help but wonder what else might be in there. Mice? Bats? Roaches?

I swallow hard, my thoughts shifting to Bellany again. When I overheard her phone conversation earlier, she told big G to meet her in the woods behind her house at nine o'clock. Since I no longer have the recording to prove Bellany is cheating, I've got to find out who big G is. There has to be a scandalous reason she is sneaking around with this guy behind Quentin's back. Otherwise, why wouldn't she just break up with him? Why keep big G a secret?

Maybe Bellany knows her father wouldn't approve, just like he disapproves of Quentin. Or what if big G already has a girlfriend? What if he has a wife? What if he's several years older than Bellany? I've got to find out who he is!

I try to envision the exterior of the house where there might be a crawl space access point. Maybe it's under the back deck, or on the side of the house near the air conditioning unit. I guess I'll just have to crawl in that hole and find out.

First I use one of Bellany's dirty shirts to wipe away the spider webs, then I shine the flashlight through the hole in the wall. All I can see is dirt, cinder blocks, more spider webs and pitch black darkness.

Be brave, I tell myself, gripping the flashlight. You can do this!

Without another moment of hesitation, I climb inside. Pointy rocks and sticks dig into my hands and knees as I crawl straight to the back of the house. Eventually, I see small slivers of light trickling through the darkness. My heart races. I found the way out!

When I make it to the vent, I attempt to pry it open with my fingers. It won't budge. As panic begins to rise inside me, I spin around, positioning my feet in front of me. *Please open, please,* I repeat in my mind as I kick the vent over and over again.

The corner finally comes loose, but only slightly. I grunt as I put more effort into each kick. *Open! Come on!* Another corner breaks free. I kick harder, hoping there's more in me to give. The metal vent squeals. Faint light bursts inside. *I did it!*

I start crawling, feeling as if I've been underwater all this time and am about to break through to the surface. I rise to my feet, gasping for air, grateful to see the vast open sky hanging above me, stars and moon shining bright. I brush myself off from head to toe, shaking my hair out, running my fingers through it, hoping I knock out any bugs or spiders. With no more time to waste, I take off racing towards the woods.

The trail feels like it goes on forever, winding through endless trees and bushes. Eventually the path splits in two different directions. I shine my light down each one. They both look like they lead to nowhere. So I head down the trail on the left, hoping luck is on my side.

The longer I'm out here in the cold, the more frustrated I feel. This is ridiculous. Why would Bellany leave her own birthday party and sneak off into the woods to meet this guy? Why not just get in her car and drive somewhere to meet him? Why come out here in the dark?

Minutes go by and the trail still stretches on, which I suspect must mean it's the wrong one. Crap! I just wasted all that time. What if they're gone now? I turn back around and head the other way, moving as fast as I can on the uneven, bumpy dirt path. The cold air continues to seep through my sweater. My nose feels like it's frozen. If it wasn't for my burning desire to get revenge, I would head straight back to the party and inside the warm house to hang out with Bridger and my friends.

Along with the leaves crackling in the wind, I soon hear cars traveling down the nearby highway. Then I see headlights coming and going, cutting through the trees. After the next bend in the path, I spot something up ahead, mixed in with the shrubs and other weeds. My pulse speeds up. That must be her! I turn off my flashlight and hide behind a tree.

Each time a set of headlights passes, I catch another glimpse of what I think might be her yellow shirt. I begin to approach slowly, struggling to see through the dark. The wind gusts, sending a shiver up my spine, only I'm not sure I'm shivering from the cold. There's something else bothering me. I don't know if I'm nervous, anxious, or what I'm experiencing exactly. I should be thrilled right now, knowing I'm about to find out who she has snuck out here to meet. So why don't I feel that way?

My stomach twists, and I hesitate to take another step. I can't shake this feeling that something's not right. A little voice inside my head tells me I should leave right now and go back to the house. But that doesn't make any sense. I'm already here. I've come all this way.

I push my doubts aside, determined to follow through with my original plan. I wait for another car to pass. As its engine roars I move to the next tree.

I'm close enough -- I need to do this now. I take a deep breath and walk straight towards her yellow shirt. "Bellany!" I call.

She doesn't respond. She doesn't move.

"Bellany, I know it's you!"

Still no response.

"Stop playing around. Get up!"

I shine my light directly at her.

What? She's alone.

I glance behind me, then turn in every direction. There's nothing but endless darkness and Bellany still isn't moving. No! It can't be! I bend down, push her hair out of her face. My stomach clenches. Blood! There's blood everywhere! What happened? Who did this to her?

"Bellany!" I shake her shoulder, scanning her body, looking for more injuries or signs for what might have happened. Her clothes are covered in dirt. Lying on the ground next to her hand is my phone. I pick it up. Was she trying to call the police for help? Where's her phone?

My back stiffens, and I nearly jump out of my shoes when a rustling noise sounds from somewhere behind me. I spin around, heart racing. "Who's there?"

The highway is eerily silent and dark. Goosebumps trail down my spine. Someone's out there.

My hand raises shakily as I point my flashlight. The noise comes again.

Run!

CHAPTER 2

Somebody killed Bellany!

My legs and lungs feel like they're burning. I'm out of breath, but I'm not going to stop running. A scream has been building in my throat, ready to explode. At any moment, I expect hands to grab a hold of me. *I don't want to die*, I repeat in my mind.

If I had seen the person who killed Bellany, I could understand them wanting to kill me too, in order to shut me up. But I didn't see anyone. It was too dark.

I run towards the bend in the path up ahead, slowing down slightly so I don't trip over the exposed tree roots. Then I speed up again.

Maybe her killer was already gone by the time I got there. Maybe nobody's chasing me. Maybe that was just the wind I heard.

The yellow haze of the house lights finally come into view. I hurdle over a thick hedge, race up the steps and burst through the back door. Once I'm inside, I push through the crowd.

I pass the dining room, the living room . . . then I hear Bridger's laugh. He's sitting on a stool in the kitchen eating one of the cupcakes I had made for him.

I move past a group of girls and head towards the counter. Wait! My feet freeze in place as a memory enters my mind of an incident that happened only a few months ago.

Bellany was in a car accident and Bridger's best friend, Terrance, was the driver of the other vehicle. I'm not convinced the accident was Terrance's fault, but Bridger believed his sister was the victim. Even though she wasn't seriously injured, Bridger still wanted revenge. He waited until Terrance got his truck fixed, then he took a bat to it, ruining the newly repaired exterior. Needless to say, they're not friends anymore.

Beads of sweat trail down my spine as I stand here looking at Bridger. Do I really want to be the one to tell him his twin sister is dead? How would I explain being out in the woods by myself? How would I explain being gone from the party all this time? He's not going to believe that Bellany locked me in the basement.

What if he thinks I killed her?

What if *everybody* thinks I killed her?

I turn on my heel, desperate to get away from Bridger, and plow right into some guy's chest. I step back and see blue frosting all over his light gray shirt. My shirt only has a couple spots on it. But the cupcake in his hand is totally smashed.

"I'm so sorry--I can get you another one," I blurt out, looking up to see who the cupcake belonged to. Blonde hair, square jaw, a one inch scar running along the top of his right eyebrow. It's Wade Toben, from Spanish class.

He stares at me for a beat with a blank expression on his face. "That was the last one."

The last one? Tears begin to swell in my eyes. I look back down at the last cupcake. It's destroyed, gone forever. Just like Bellany.

Wade clears his throat. "It's not a big deal, Charlotte. It's just a cupcake."

"It's ruined," I whisper. All of the noises in the house -- the people talking, laughing, music playing -- it all falls silent as my mind flashes back to what happened outside when I saw Bellany lying there in the dirt and leaves, her hair a tangled mess, matted with blood.

I didn't want Bellany to die. No matter how much I hated her, I didn't want *this* to happen. How could someone murder her -- brutally murder her?

Was she caught by surprise? Did she know her attacker?

Did big G kill her?

She was out there in the dark. By herself. In the cold. Her last few minutes of life were probably terrifying. I clamp my eyes shut, realizing I can't let myself grieve for her. I can't be sad! Not now. Not ever! I'm afraid if I continue to let myself feel these emotions, I might go insane!

A hand rests on my shoulder. "Charlotte?" Wade prompts.

I pull away and race up the stairs.

When I reach the end of the hall, I burst through the bathroom door and lock myself inside. My legs feel wobbly. I collapse onto the floor, in shock, not sure what to do.

Eventually, I realize I'm still holding the flashlight and I'm so eager to get rid of it, I open a random drawer and toss it inside.

I don't have an alibi for Bellany's time of death. And as for a motive, that's an easy question to answer. Hate. My friends Gemma and Vivy know all about my history with Bellany. And they're not the only ones. Several other people at school know we're enemies, including faculty members.

No alibi, plus a motive . . . this isn't good. I look guilty!

I know what I have to do. I have to play it cool, get back out there and join the party. That's what an innocent person would do, right?

Hopefully the real murderer was careless enough to leave behind some DNA or something. Hold on. Did I leave anything out there? I check my pockets to make sure I still have my phone.

"Charlotte!" an unfamiliar high-pitched voice calls from the other side of the door. "Are you done yet?"

"Just a minute." I look down at the fluffy bath rug I'm sitting on, then something strange catches my eye. There's a reddish-brown smudge on my shoe. Dirt? I squint and lean closer. My heart races. Is that . . . blood?

I spring to my feet, snatch a washcloth from the shelf and douse it with soap and water. Why did I wear my white Converse tonight? Of all the shoes I could have chosen, I chose white!

After vigorous scrubbing, the stain still isn't coming out.

A knock comes to the door. "Charlotte!"

I look under the sink for some kind of bathroom cleaner, hoping to find bleach. There's nothing there. I search through the drawers, scan the counter top: Brush, soap, lotion, tube of toothpaste. Hold on. That might work. I snatch up the toothpaste and pop off the cap. It's white! This is perfect! I smear a generous glob over the blood stain, working it into the fabric. It's not gone, but at least the stain doesn't look like blood anymore.

I wash my hands with soap and scalding hot water, trying not to freak out about having touched Bellany's blood.

The door bangs. "Hurry up!" several voices shout.

"Just a second!"

One last look in the mirror to make sure I'm presentable. I fluff my hair, ignoring the fact that my curls have gone flat from being outside. At least my waterproof mascara stayed on. I take a deep breath. Exhale. *You can do this.*

There's a long line of people waiting. Standing at the front is a girl with straight blonde hair, blunt cut bangs and braces on her teeth. She's glaring at me as if I have just stolen money from her grandmother. "So inconsiderate, Charlotte!" Her shoulder bumps against mine. Door slams.

"Excuse you!" I snap.

Who is that girl? How does she know my name? And what makes her think she can talk to me like that?

"Wow," someone chuckles.

I turn around and find Vivy Bailey standing in line with a smirk on her face. Vivy had a falling-out with her old group of friends a couple of months ago, so I invited her to hang out with me and my friends. She seems to fit in fine, except I'm still waiting for her to give up on her old habit of wearing *all black*.

Vivy checks the screen on her phone. "You were in there for ten minutes and thirty-eight seconds."

She was timing me? Seriously? I didn't think I was in there that long. But I needed every single second to prepare myself to come out here and face everybody. Pulling off the innocent act when I have first-hand knowledge about the murder of

Smithfield-Selma High School's most popular girl would be a challenge for even the most talented actor, I'm sure. But this is self-preservation motivating me.

Vivy reaches inside the collar of her shirt, tugging her bra strap back up onto her shoulder. "I thought maybe you were in there with someone," she says with a smirk.

The bathroom door swings open and the blonde girl comes out. My eyes sweep across her silky choral-colored shirt, her black leggings, then her feet. Wait, what? She's not wearing any shoes. I point so Vivy can see. "What in the world?"

Vivy raises an eyebrow. I think she's impressed by the girl's boldness.

"Who is that?" I ask. "She knows my name, but I have never seen her before."

"I don't know. She's been hanging all over Bridger tonight. Flirting, big time."

My mind suddenly discards any concerns about the rude blonde girl, and freezes at the mention of Bridger's name. He is going to absolutely lose his mind when he finds out his twin sister is dead and that it happened on their seventeenth birthday.

The line moves up again. Vivy's complaining about how bad the bathroom downstairs smells, which is why everybody wants to use this one.

I'm not really paying attention to what she's saying. I'm trying to figure out if I should confide in her. I don't think Vivy would freak out to hear that Bellany's dead. The concern I have is whether I can trust her to keep her mouth shut.

"So where have you been all night?" she asks. "Besides camping out in the bathroom."

My stomach dips with sudden nervousness. Should I tell her? Vivy runs her fingers across her forehead, pushing her long, wavy black hair out of her face. No. I don't know her well enough. I can't tell her. I can't tell anybody.

My eyes scan the crowded hallway. There are so many people here. It would be easy for me to blend in, right? And the lights are dimmed. Vivy should believe me if I tell her I've been here the entire night. "Oh, you know." I shrug. "I've been around."

"I'm surprised I haven't run into queen B, yet." *Queen B* is Vivy's nickname for Bellany. She's looking at me, waiting for me to comment. But I'm not going to join in the Bellany bashing right now, or ever again. I pull out my phone and stare down at the screen, desperate to clear my mind from the horrifying image of Bellany's dead body that won't stop replaying in my head.

The line finally moves again.

"I'll be downstairs," I say, about to leave.

"I'm gonna stay up here." Vivy nods toward a guy with tattoos and piercings.

"Oh. Okay." Maybe it's a good thing that Vivy won't be hanging out with me. I don't want her to suspect that something's wrong. The less time we spend together the better.

As I weave through the crowd in the hallway, I pass by Bellany's bedroom door and suddenly I can't breathe. My legs feel like jello. Everything around me turns into a blurr. Bodies bump against me. People are talking. I can't make out what they're saying.

Desperate to get out of here, I somehow make it down the stairs and find my way to the front door. I burst through it, practically tripping over my own feet. Cold air hits. My lungs finally expand, taking in the chill. I wander over to the far end of the porch and collapse onto one of the rocking chairs, burying my face into my hands. *Don't cry. Just breathe.*

Voices come and go around me. Footsteps enter and exit the house, while I sit here and wonder if I made the right decision. What if it's days before her body is found?

It was two weeks before Grandma was discovered. A neighbor found her. She had died of a heart attack, in her home, by herself. I was eleven-years-old at the time. Mom and I had just moved clear across the country, from Oregon to North Carolina. It was Grandma who taught me how to bake cookies, cakes, pies, breads. I still miss her, even though she died five years ago.

I rock back and forth, staring up at the full moon in the sky. The cold wind gusts, and I welcome the numb feeling in my fingers and toes. If only it could dull this pain I'm feeling in my chest.

I turn my head and look at the three jack-o'-lanterns sitting clustered together near the front door, lights flickering inside. Bridger and I carved those last week. We were having a good time until Bellany came into the kitchen. She yelled at us for making a mess.

As soon as we finished carving, Bridger went outside to take the pumpkin guts to the garbage can. That's when Bellany came back into the kitchen. She was talking on her phone. "Okay. I'll call you later, big goober." She lowered her phone and looked right at me, the smile gone from her face. "You know Bridger's never going to like you as anything more than a friend. He tells me that all the time. He said you're too plain vanilla looking and you don't have any curves. He's not attracted to you--*at all*. Nobody is."

I didn't care that Bridger wasn't attracted to me -- we are friends and that's it. I have no other interest in him. What bothered me was her commentary on my appearance.

She then nudged the plate of snickerdoodle cookies I made, wrinkled up her nose and narrowed her eyes until the pale blue color disappeared and all I could see were black pupils. "Most of the stuff you bake for Bridger goes straight into the garbage can. He's just too nice to tell you he doesn't want all this junk. It tastes disgusting."

I knew she was deliberately trying to destroy my self-esteem and I shouldn't listen to her. Yet, I couldn't help but wonder if what she said might be true. Did Bridger throw away the food I baked for him? Did it not taste amazing?

I looked up from the plate of cookies, seeing the smirk on her face, and something inside me snapped. I reached across the table, picked up a cookie and acted like I was about to take a bite but instead I threw it at her. It hit her right in the face. A half second later, Bridger walked back into the kitchen, unaware of what just happened. Bellany stormed off without retaliating, but I knew she would get back at me later. And she did.

Another gust of wind blows, bringing my thoughts back to the present. Just then, walking up the steps of the front porch, I see my best friend, Gemma Hernandez. She sent me a text earlier saying she was on restriction and couldn't come tonight. Yet here she is, gift in hand, wearing a long black coat which must be covering up a dress or a skirt since her legs are bare, and she's also wearing a pair of black five inch high heels. Why is she so dressed up, I wonder. Gemma is only four feet, eleven inches tall, so wearing heels makes a huge difference for her.

"Did your mom change her mind?" I ask, wondering if she's going to stick around for a while.

"I wish." Gemma rolls her eyes. She holds up a shiny blue gift bag with a silver bow. "I convinced her to let me come and drop this off for Bridger." She breathes out a heavy sigh. "But I can't stay."

When we get inside, Gemma takes off her coat and tosses it over the banister. I stare at what she's wearing, wondering if maybe Vivy might be rubbing off on her. Gemma's dress looks like something worn at a funeral. "You're wearing all black," I say.

"So?"

"Well, you just . . ." I hesitate, trying to think of a way to say this without insulting her. Then I notice how thick her black eyeliner is, just like Vivy's. "Normally you wear color."

Gemma's mouth drops open. I follow her gaze over to the couch where Bridger is sitting with his arm draped around the rude blonde girl. "Who is that?"

"I don't know. Just some snob," I say, remembering how she called me inconsiderate for taking too long in the bathroom and then purposely bumped into my shoulder.

Gemma's dark brown eyes turn glossy, filling with tears, which surprises me. She has seen Bridger with other girls before. This kind of thing happens all the time.

"I can't deal with this tonight." She pivots back towards the door, ankles wobble.

"What's the matter?"

"I'm just tired of this." She grabs her coat.

"Hold on." I take the gift bag from her, knowing she will regret not leaving it for Bridger. "Is there a card or a note, so he'll know it's from you?"

"Yeah, there's a note," she sniffs. "But don't give it to him in front of *her*." She shoots a dirty look over to the blonde.

"I wasn't gonna."

Gemma wipes a black tear from her cheek, but there's still a streak of black eyeliner left on her face. She follows a group of people out the door.

Gemma is pretty, curvy, and she's smart and sassy. Which is exactly Bridger's type. But he has never shown interest in her. We suspect Bellany must have somehow ruined her chances with him. There is no other reason we can think of for him to keep her in the friend zone.

After I drop the gift bag off in Bridger's bedroom, I head back to the living room. Since all the couches and chairs are occupied, I remove a lamp from an end table and take a seat there.

As I watch the people around me, I start to feel uneasy and nervous again, wondering if I should still be here. Maybe I should leave, like Gemma did. What if it's *not* days before Bellany's body is discovered, what if it's discovered tonight? Do I really want to be here when that happens?

Nervous, anxious, scary thoughts continue to race through my mind as I sit here pretending like I'm having a good time.

Minutes pass, maybe hours.

Have I been here long enough? Is it fine for me to leave now?

"Charlotte!" a deep voice calls, making my heart constrict. Quentin Colson is heading straight towards me, his Duke baseball cap hovering several inches higher than everybody else in the room. I cross my ankles to hide my stained shoe, as the crowd willingly parts to let Bellany's boyfriend through.

Now I know I should have already left.

That secret, about Bellany cheating on him, doesn't mean anything now. It only mattered if Bellany was still around so he could break up with her. But he's never going to see her again. And I'm never going to tell him she cheated. If I did, he would think I'm some kind of a heartless monster. The last thing I want to do is give him a reason to hate me.

CHAPTER 3

Quentin's chocolate brown eyes hold my gaze, and it's like someone is shining a spotlight on my face. What if he suspects something is wrong with me and starts asking questions? I don't think I have a strong enough poker face to endure an interrogation right now.

"Have you seen Bellany?" he asks.

All of the oxygen feels like it's being sucked out of the air. *Have I seen Bellany?* I know the answer I must give him, but it's a lie. Is he going to believe me? "I haven't seen her in a while."

His eyes travel across the room, then land on me again. "Can you scoot over?"

My mind begins to race with possible excuses so I can leave. But before I come up with something, he sits down next to me. His long legs sprawl out leaving no extra space between us. My stomach flutters. Normally I would love sitting close to him like this.

He pulls out his phone, tapping the screen to check for messages. "When I call her, it goes straight to voicemail. And she's not returning my texts. Do you have any idea where she might be?"

"Um--" I begin to cough. My throat is so dry I can't help it. What am I gonna say? I scoot back, sitting up straighter. "Hmm . . ." I put my thinking face on. "Have you searched every single room in the house? Even upstairs?"

His gaze shifts over to the staircase. Several people are sitting there, leaving only a small pathway to walk through. "I've searched the entire house. Maybe I should go look in the backyard, in the woods."

A chill goes through me as my focus turns to the windows at the back of the house and the dark, foreboding sky outside. Bellany's body is close to the trail. Lights from vehicles passing by on the highway help brighten up the area. He should be able to find her, and then I won't have to worry about being the first person who discovered her dead body. Quentin will be the unfortunate one. Wait! That would be a disaster! Bellany's dead body . . . found by her boyfriend! The cops will suspect he's the one who killed her. They always suspect the boyfriend!

Quentin sits forward, about to get up. "Text me if she shows up while I'm gone."

I grab hold of his arm. "I know where you should look for her. Out front! Maybe she's hanging out with someone in their car, or maybe she went for a walk." Quentin's determined expression doesn't change. I've got to try harder to convince him. "Think about it," I say, squeezing his arm. "What would she be doing out walking in the woods? In the dark? It's like super spooky out there." I shake my head. "I bet she's out front, where everybody's coming and going. She probably went out there to meet someone. Or maybe she's on her way back from going somewhere. Like the store. If she is, then you'll find her out front, where all the cars are."

Quentin scratches his head, thinking. I know he's worried something's wrong with Bellany, so it makes sense he would want to look for her out back. That's where something bad would happen, because there's nobody around to be a witness -- no one close enough to hear a bloodcurdling scream.

"Come on," I say. "Let's go out front. I'll help you look for her." I nod, hoping he'll agree.

"Do you have a coat?" he asks.

"I think I left it at school today," I reply like it isn't a big deal. I actually don't know where I last left it. But that doesn't matter. What matters is that I go with him and make sure he stays far away from the back of the house, even if it means I freeze outside.

"I saw you when you arrived at school today. You weren't wearing a coat."

Was he really paying that close attention? "Oh, right. Maybe I left it at school yesterday."

"How many coats have you lost this school year?"

I shrug, even though I'm aware I've lost four.

He takes his coat off and wraps it around my shoulders. "Here. You're gonna need this. I can tell you're cold. You're shivering."

I am? I know I'm nervous, but I didn't realize I was shaking. "Thank you." I fold my arms across my chest as if I'm trying to warm up. His coat is huge. It's like I'm wearing a tent, but I'm glad he loaned it to me. It smells like his woodsy cologne.

"Just don't lose it." He gives me a soft smile.

"I won't," I promise. "We should check through all of the parked cars. Who knows -- she might be hanging out in one of them." I tug his arm and lead him to the front door.

We use our phones as flashlights and begin searching through the cars parked in the driveway. Then we head to the street. Despite my effort to be super slow and drag this out, Quentin is moving at a fast, urgent pace.

I zip up his coat, high on my neck to keep warm as the wind gusts. Leaves crackle, tumbling across the ground and over my feet.

Quentin walks across the street towards a white BMW. He shines his light in the driver's side window, which promptly rolls down a couple inches.

"What's your problem!" shouts an irritated, deep voice.

Quentin swiftly moves around to the passenger side window.

"Get out of here!" the voice shouts again.

"Quentin, come on," I say.

He finishes checking each window before walking away.

"Who was that?" I ask him.

"No idea. I've never seen them before."

We head over to the next vehicle. Not only is Quentin

being quick with his inspection, he's also extremely thorough, looking in every window and opening doors. He bends down and presses his ear against the trunk of a car.

"What are you doing?" I ask.

"I thought I heard something."

"Heard what?"

Quentin remains quiet and doesn't respond. "Anybody in there?" he shouts. Another few seconds go by in silence. "I guess it was nothing." He turns and walks towards a tall truck parked across the street.

"You thought Bellany was in the trunk?" I ask, surprised.

He pulls up a tarp that's covering the bed of the truck and starts rummaging through things. "There's a lot of psychos in the world, Charlotte. You never know what they might do to someone."

Guilt begins to thicken inside me. Somehow I need to wipe the images of Bellany's dead body from my mind. I have to forget the truth.

I watch Quentin. I try to tap into his urgency, his concern, and that thread of hope he's clinging to that we'll find Bellany any minute now safe and sound. I try to manufacture those same feelings. I've always heard if you repeat a lie enough times you can begin to believe it. I sure hope that's true.

Eventually we finish checking all the vehicles on the west side of Bellany and Bridger's house. We turn back around and walk down the street in the other direction, passing Quentin's royal blue, classic Camaro. We don't stop to look inside it. He claims his car is always locked, so we don't need to waste our time.

Several vehicles later, we arrive at my decrepit 1978 Ford Bronco. The light from my phone shines up at a large oak tree a few feet away, and I realize something's not right. "I thought I parked closer to the house than this," I say as I open the door and climb inside. My knees bang against the dash. "What in the world?" Reaching for the lever, I scoot my seat back to the right spot. When I look up, I notice the rearview mirror is angled toward the ceiling. "I think somebody drove my car." But why? Who?

Quentin walks around to the passenger side. The door creaks as it swings open. "Did you leave your keys inside or something?"

"No." I reach in my pocket, pull my keys out. "They're right here."

He stares at me with a knowing look in his eyes.

"What?"

"You and your keys." He shakes his head. "Do you have any idea how many car keys you have lost in one month? I open my mouth to respond, but he cuts me off. "Three." He's making me sound like an airhead, which I don't like. Lots of people lose their keys -- I'm not the only one. But what bothers me the most, is he knows the exact number of times this has happened. "So you're keeping track?" I ask with slight irritation in my tone.

"My point is," he says dismissively. "It shouldn't be a surprise that someone took your Bronco for a joyride."

"Well, it is a surprise. Just because someone found one of my keys, doesn't give them the right to steal my car. A crime has been committed." I bite my lip, realizing I shouldn't bring up the subject of crimes.

Quentin takes a quick inventory of the Bronco's interior, his gaze ricocheting around from one imperfection to another -- faded dash, drooping headliner, ripped upholstery. "At least they brought it back," he mumbles. "Is anything missing?"

There really isn't anything valuable in here to steal. Phone charger, chapstick, spare change. . . . "I don't think so."

"Maybe we should check the exterior for new dents."

"New dents? This Bronco is covered with dents and scratches. How am I supposed to know if there's a new one? Why do people think they can take something that doesn't belong to them?" My voice continues to rise. I'm losing control of my emotions. This was a mistake to come out here with Quentin. I can't pretend like everything's fine. I can't pretend like I didn't see Bellany's dead body!

A bright set of headlights shine through the back window. My stomach dips when I see the vehicle pass. It's a deputy sheriff cruiser. I watch in silence as the red tail lights move further down the street. *They found her!*

Quentin crumples his hat in his hands. He has the same look in his eyes that he gets when he's playing basketball with seconds left on the clock and his team is down by a couple points. "Let's go back to the house and see what's going on."

I get out and shut the door as if I'm going to follow him, but my feet remain glued to the street. I don't need to protect Quentin anymore. He can go back there if he wants.

Quentin stops suddenly, noticing I'm not at his side. "You coming?"

I place my hand over my stomach -- a move I had done several times before to get out of running during PE class. "Cramps," I say, wincing. "Go ahead. I'll catch up."

He quickly returns. "I'll walk slow so you can keep up."

Another set of headlights approach, and we move out of the way. My breathing quickens when I see the lettering on the side of the vehicle. It's another cop car, driving much faster than the previous one. It passes by, leaving a plume of dust in the air.

"Charlotte . . ." Quentin's voice shutters. "What if something happened to her?"

I wonder how he's going to handle the bad news when he finds out. Will it break him? Will he be strong enough to keep living his life and pursuing his dreams? "I-I'm sure she's fine." He hooks his arm around mine in an attempt to pull me along. "I can't. My stomach is really cramping. You go ahead. I'll meet you back there," I lie, determined not to go back at all.

"What kind of a friend would I be if I left you out here by yourself in the dark?"

"Quentin," I sigh. "I'm not helpless, you know. I can take care of myself."

The corners of his mouth turn down. "I know you can. But I don't want to have to worry about you *and* Bellany."

My heart melts a little. *He would worry about me?*

"Charlotte," he says quietly. "Why do I have the feeling I'm never going to see her again?"

Realizing how grief-stricken he is almost takes my breath away. It's too painful to see him hurting like this. I start walking with him, pull out my phone and look down at the screen, trying to hide my glossy eyes.

"Do you think I'm wrong?" he asks. "Is there some kind of rational explanation for her being gone that I'm not thinking of?"

I clamp my eyes shut for a moment as I lower my phone, wondering what I could possibly say to provide him any comfort. When I open my eyes again, I catch sight of my stained shoe in the light from my phone. Seeing this instantly awakens my survival instinct to fight for control of the emotional avalanche cascading inside me, nearly at its breaking point.

A couple guys come running towards us like they've just broken out of jail. One of them is Ace. He's not running as fast as his friend. He has one hand on his pants, trying to keep them from falling down. "Look who it is." Ace grins at me. "You want to come party with me and Stew?" He points to the guy next to him, then nods at Quentin. "Sup!"

Ace seems a little off, not like his usual self. I wonder if he's drunk or maybe he's high.

"Hey," Quentin says. "What's going on back there?"

I'm just as anxious as Quentin is to find out what's going on at the Silverfield's house. I shine my light at Ace, but I avoid his eyes so I don't blind him.

Ace gives his pants another tug. "I dunno, man," he replies, slurring his words. "We took off when we saw the cops. I was like, dude, let's hop the back fence and get outta here."

The front pocket of Ace's shirt, the one he had his phone stuffed in earlier is ripped and hanging by a few threads. I wonder if maybe he caught it on the fence when he was ditching the cops.

Ace's friend, Stew, starts to walk away. "Yo, let's go."

"So you don't know what the cops wanted?" I ask again to

clarify before they leave. "You didn't hear anything?"

Ace grins as if he's amused. "I don't know, babe. They probably want what every cop wants when they break up a party full of teenagers -- to bust 'em for underage drinking." He laughs, buckling over. My light shines on the side of his face. There are some scratches on his cheek. Did he get those from climbing the fence, too?

"What happened?" I point. "You're bleeding."

"What happened with what?" he replies, standing there swaying.

"You have some scratches on your cheek."

Stew busts out laughing. "He biffed it and face-planted into the bushes. I told him to pull his pants up or he'd fall."

I'm relieved to hear the explanation, because I couldn't help but wonder if maybe the marks on his face had come from a girl's fingernails -- as in Bellany's fingernails. I bet she tried to fight off her attacker.

"Let's go!" Stew demands again.

"Charlotte," Ace says to me, ignoring his friend. "Come with us. I promise you'll have a good time. And I'll keep my hands to myself."

I shoot him a look of disgust. "I don't think so."

"She's staying with me," Quentin snaps.

Ace grabs hold of his belt and runs off after Stew. "Man, how far did you park?"

Quentin is staring at me strangely. "What?" I ask him.

"Ace said he'll keep his hands to himself. Why did he say that? Has he done something to you in the past?"

"No!" I shake my head. "He's just drunk."

A car's engine rumbles, but there are no headlights shining. Suddenly it pulls up alongside us, and Quentin promptly flashes his light at the window as it rolls down.

Wade is sitting behind the wheel. I'm remembering the cupcake I smashed into his shirt and how I practically burst into tears right in front of him.

I had heard that Wade moved to North Carolina at the

start of the school year. But I don't know where he moved from, or much else about him either. We've never really talked until tonight.

Quentin leans forward to peer inside his vehicle, which I now realize is a black Dodge Charger that looks like an unmarked cop car. "Are you leaving because of the police?" Quentin asks. "Do you know what they want?"

"They closed off the house and won't let anybody leave." Wade looks directly at me. "I wouldn't go back there if I were you." He pauses for a beat. "Do you need a ride?"

"No." I point to my Bronco. "My car's right here."

Quentin rests his hand on the roof of Wade's Charger. "How did you--" The engine roars, interrupting him. He jumps out of the way as the Charger takes off. Quentin looks ticked, but he doesn't say anything.

The key to my Bronco is already in my hand. I'm beyond anxious to get out of here. "Do what you want to do, Quentin, but I'm going home."

"Wait. What if this has something to do with Bellany? Aren't you going to come with me back to the house to find out?"

"Sorry--I just--I can't." I turn back to my Bronco, feeling like I'm the worst friend in the world. I'm lying to Quentin, and I'm leaving him alone to discover that the girl he's in love with has just been murdered. I hope he never finds out the truth; that I knew all along what happened to her.

By the time I get home, my phone is blowing up with text messages and other notifications. I race up to my bedroom and sit on my bed, ready to sift through every single message and social media post. Then I hear Mom's slippers sliding across the floor in the hallway.

She leans against the door frame with an inquisitive smile. Her auburn hair is pulled up in a messy bun, makeup off, wearing leggings and an oversized T-shirt. I wonder if I woke her. She probably didn't expect me to come home at all tonight.

Mom opens her mouth, but instead of speaking, she yawns first. "Did Bridger like the cupcakes you made him?"

"Yeah." At least I think he did. He was eating them.

"Did you have a good time?"

I nod and force a smile.

She sits down on the edge of my bed and starts reminiscing about the parties she went to when she was my age -- I've heard all these stories before.

Normally I tell her everything, because she never judges or lectures me. But then again, I haven't really ever done anything that bad. I think Mom tries to be more of a friend to me than a mother, because she feels bad for leaving me home alone several days in a row each time she's away for work.

But I'm too ashamed to tell her what happened tonight. What would she think of me if she were to find out I didn't help Bellany? I can just imagine the kinds of questions she would ask me: *Did you perform CPR? Were you able to revive her?* Then I would have to admit I did nothing. I didn't even call 9-1-1. Whoa. Now that I think about it, I didn't check her pulse either. My stomach dips. What if Bellany was still alive, and I could have saved her? The term *negligent homicide* comes to my mind. I learned about this from watching massive amounts of crime scene investigation shows.

Or, maybe she's not dead. Maybe she regained consciousness and drug herself to the road, then someone stopped to help her. Is that why the cops showed up? Because they were looking for the person who attacked her?

"Are you okay, honey?"

I snap out of my thoughts and force another smile on my face. "Yeah. I'm fine. I'm just tired." I squeeze my phone in my hand, dying to swipe the screen and find out what's going on back at Bridger's house. Another ding goes off -- a text message notification.

Mom yawns. "I'm tired too. I've got a lot of errands to run tomorrow. Which reminds me, I need you to make a list of grocery items you want from the store. A week's worth, because I won't be back until next Sunday." She pauses and yawns again just before walking out the door. "I've also got a lot of studying

I need to do tomorrow." Mom teaches computer certification classes and is always trying to stay up to date with the latest in technology.

"I could run errands for you tomorrow, so you can study," I offer.

"Sounds great. I'll make a list and text it to you," she says, turning to leave.

As soon as the door closes, I flip my phone over. There's a message from Vivy. **QUEEN B IS DEAD!!!!!!!!!**

The next one is from Gemma. **Someone MURDERED Bellany!**

I pause instead of reading on, feeling sick to my stomach. My question has been answered. Bellany didn't survive.

Am I to blame for this? Could I have saved her? No. I refuse to believe it was my fault. I had to run away. I couldn't have stayed there. Her killer might have been lingering around. He could have tried to kill me too.

I head to the bathroom and turn on the shower. As I stand under the hot water, I try to convince myself I'm not a bad person. I did what anybody in my situation would have done. I grab the bar of soap and lather it in my hands.

If I had an alibi for Bellany's time of death, I would have called for help and told Bridger. It's Bellany's fault that I don't have anyone to vouch for my whereabouts. She's the one who locked me in the basement. She's the one who placed me in this impossible situation. And besides, she should have never left her party. It's her fault she's dead. Not mine!

I get out of the shower, dry off and twist my hair up in a towel. I stand in front of the sink, staring at my reflection in the mirror and groan. I look sick. My face is pale. There are dark circles under my eyes.

I smile, wondering if it looks genuine or forced. I change my expression to one of surprise, then sadness. The next time I'm around Quentin and Bridger, I'm going to have to pretend to be sad. I hope they'll believe me.

My mouth opens, eyes widen. "I can't believe she's really

gone." I repeat this sentence again a few more times, adjusting my tone of voice until I'm somewhat satisfied with the result. At least tomorrow is Saturday. I have the weekend to prepare myself for the onslaught of discussion, gossip and mayhem that will take place at school on Monday. I'm sure there will be plenty of tears shed over Bellany's tragic death. But not by me. I draw the line at fake crying -- no way I'm gonna do that.

CHAPTER 4

I'm sitting on a hard and severely uncomfortable church pew as the organ bellows, playing an unfamiliar hymn. Mom and I haven't been to church since we moved to North Carolina five years ago. I don't know why we stopped going, since we used to go with Grandma every week when we lived back in Oregon.

But I'm not here for church service. I'm here for Bellany's funeral.

Eight days have gone by since she was murdered. The cops still don't know who killed her. So I'm full of anxiety, constantly worrying it's just a matter of time before someone points a finger at me.

My gaze lowers to my feet. I'm wearing high heel shoes that pinch my toes, borrowed them from Mom. I slip my feet out and exhale in relief. But my shoes aren't the only thing bothering me. This ruffled shirt I'm wearing is making me sweat, despite having applied two coats of deodorant. In my hand, I'm holding a white handkerchief with my initials on it. CG, for Charlotte Gray. Mom insisted I bring this to Bellany's funeral, but I doubt I'll be needing it. I'm not sad.

Gemma is sitting next to me, decked out in black, wearing the same dress that she wore to the party. Her legs are crossed, foot bouncing. I think she's uncomfortable too. "Will they be doing an open casket?" she asks, voice low. "I wonder what she looks like." Gemma wrinkles up her nose. "Her face must be all . . . you know . . . pale and stuff." She shutters.

I don't have to try very hard to imagine what Bellany might look like. I saw Bellany's face the night she died. And I really wish I could forget what it looked like. The image haunts me, especially at night when I try to sleep. I shake my head. "Bridger told me they aren't going to do an open casket."

Gemma fans herself with the program. Her dark hair is pulled up in a ponytail. A few loose strands hang down around her face and flutter in the breeze. "The coroner has obviously completed the autopsy since they're going to bury her today," she says. "So why hasn't Bridger told us how she died? Or Quentin? Friends are supposed to share things like that. Deep, secret things. Don't these boys know that?"

Since when do boys willingly share secrets, I want to say, but I don't. "Bridger told me his dad won't reveal the initial findings of the autopsy with him until after the funeral. So if Bridger doesn't know how Bellany died, then Quentin doesn't know either." I can't tell Gemma my theory about how she died. Based on what I saw, which was a lot of blood, I think she was beaten to death.

Gemma's still cringing in disgust. "It must be something really bad, maybe gory or gruesome." She quickly looks around at the people nearby. "What if her murderer is here?"

My gut twists. I can feel the wet fabric of my shirt clinging to my armpits. Hearing Gemma speculate about who might have killed Bellany and how they did it, is starting to make me feel sick. I wish I could tell her I stumbled across Bellany's dead body the night of the party, but then she would have to keep that information a secret, and I'm not sure she would be able to. She's not good at keeping secrets.

When we were in middle school, I liked this boy named Gabe Sanchez. Long story short, Bellany found out and deliberately swooped in and stole him from me. I was hurt and furious and wanted to get back at her, so I wrote on the girls bathroom mirror and on each bathroom stall door, **Bellany IS A BOYFRIEND STEALER**, with a permanent marker. Rumors went around school about who wrote it and eventually the principal questioned several girls in my class, including Gemma. She said she tried to lie for me, but she was too intimidated by our principal, so she ratted me out. If Gemma couldn't handle a principal's interrogation, she definitely wouldn't be able to handle questioning from the cops.

Gemma nudges my arm. Her eyes signal for me to turn and look at the entrance of the chapel. Quentin's mom, Ruby Colson, has just arrived. I don't think I have ever seen her wear a dress before. Her usual attire consists of yoga pants and a tank top. Sometimes I envision her in an orange jumpsuit. It's kind of hard not to, since I know about her past. I researched her name and read everything printed about her. I also watched the news clips. Ruby's method of killing her husband was poison. She slipped it right into his mashed potatoes and gravy, which sounds more like premeditation was involved than self defense, as she had claimed. The jury obviously thought that too since they convicted her of first-degree murder.

My eyes quickly scan through the crowd surrounding her. I wonder where Quentin is. I haven't heard from him since the party. He hasn't replied to a single one of my texts or phone calls. He hasn't been back to school.

Gemma and I stopped by his house to check on him a couple days ago, but we weren't invited inside. Ruby met us at the door and said Quentin wasn't up to having any visitors. So we left a plate of brownies I had baked -- since those are his favorite -- along with a sympathy card.

I'm surprised his mom is here. Just like Mr. Silverfield, she didn't approve of Quentin and Bellany's relationship. She thought Bellany demanded too much of Quentin's time -- time she thought he could better spend by practicing basketball or doing school work. His grades took a dive when they started going out and haven't recovered.

"I'm going to go talk to her," I say as I slip my shoes back on. I hope Quentin is around here somewhere.

"Hi, Ms. Colson," I say with a smile. But I make sure my smile isn't too big. I don't want her to think I'm insensitive about this whole *murder* situation. Or maybe she doesn't care if I look happy. For all I know, she may be relieved that Bellany's dead.

"Hello, Charlotte." Her tone is a little strained, like she's uncomfortable. I guess we have that in common.

"Is Quentin here?" I ask.

"We drove separately." She runs her fingers through her curled dark hair. Normally she would have it pulled back in a braid.

"So how's he doing?"

She sighs, worry lines creasing her forehead. "I told him he has to go back to school. The basketball team is depending on him, and he has scholarships on the line." Her lips purse together in a tight line. "He should have never gotten mixed up with Bellany. I knew she would be bad for him."

I'm surprised to hear her speak so candidly and negatively about Bellany while at her funeral. Of course, I agree with her one-hundred percent, but I don't think I should admit it. I turn and look across the room, unsure how to respond.

Ruby leans in close. "Quentin's under a lot of stress," she whispers, eyes locked onto mine. "The detectives have questioned him several times about the night Bellany died. Have they questioned you?"

Me? Why would they question me? Does she know something? Have the cops shared any of their theories with her? "No," I say, hoping I sound calm and cool, like I have nothing to hide.

She blinks as if she's confused, forehead wrinkles. "But you were at the party, right?"

There were tons of people at the party. "Yeah, I was there. But I left before the cops arrived."

"Hmm." She pauses for a beat. "I bet a lot of girls were jealous of Bellany. They probably even hated her. She seemed to have everything going for her. She was pretty, a cheerleader, smart, and she was dating my son . . . she must have had enemies."

Ruby's looking at me strangely, and I can't help but wonder if she's accusing me of being one of Bellany's enemies. How would she know that?

"Can you think of anyone who might have wanted to harm Bellany?" she asks, eyes intently holding my gaze.

Is she serious? She wants me to name names? There's no way I'm doing that. "I can't think of anybody," I say, again trying to act innocent, hoping I'm successful. "I sure wish the detectives would leave Quentin alone. He would never have harmed Bellany."

The crease between her eyebrows disappears. She takes a deep breath. "Well, if you hear anything that might help point the detectives in the right direction, please let me know, and I'll pass it along to them. You will do that, won't you?" Her request doesn't sound like a question. She's insisting.

"Oh definitely." I nod. "I'll keep my ears open. Whatever I can do to help."

"Thank you, hun." Her attention is drawn to a group of people entering the chapel. She frowns. "I better find a seat in the back, before they're all taken."

I watch her walk away and can't help but feel concerned and confused about what she thinks of me. Does she not trust me? I'm her son's ally. If it wasn't for me, Quentin might be behind bars right now. I'm the one who made sure he stayed away from the woods that night.

The minister stands at the front of the chapel. I think he's waiting for everybody to be seated so the funeral can start. I quickly head back to my seat.

Gemma and I watch people filter into the pews around us. This place is nearly filled to capacity, mostly with people from school.

Her fingers suddenly clamp down on my arm. "There's Wade Toben." She bites her lip watching him. He's so hot!"

Casually, I steal a glance as Wade walks down the aisle. When he's far enough in front of us, I let my eyes linger. He looks good in a suit. It accentuates his broad shoulders. If I didn't already know he's a sophomore in high school like me, I'd probably peg him as a college student. He has a mature vibe about him, and it's kind of hard to pinpoint where it comes from . . . maybe it's the confident way he carries himself.

I lean in close to Gemma so only she can hear. "He offered to give me a ride home from Bridger and Bellany's party."

Her eyes bulge, fingers squeeze harder. I pull my arm out of her death grip. "Did you go with him?"

"No. I drove my Bronco there. I didn't need a ride."

She gives me a sympathetic sigh. "What a bummer. If I were you, I would have lied and said I didn't drive. I would have hopped right into his car. Who knows what you might have missed out on. Maybe you'd be sitting next to him right now."

"I doubt that."

Her attention is drawn to someone else. "Oh look, there's Samantha. . . ."

I continue staring at Wade's tousled blonde hair and chiseled profile, zoning out, not really listening to Gemma comment on who else has just walked in. The chapel is becoming noisy, but I'm not registering what other people around me are saying either. I'm only focusing on Wade. I wonder what he thinks of me. Was he just being polite to offer me a ride home? Could he possibly be interested in me?

Wade turns and looks, catching me in full stare. Crud. My cheeks begin to burn.

Gemma nudges my arm again. I'm grateful for the interruption. "Who wears white to a funeral?" she gasps as she shoots a dirty look over to the side of the chapel.

Turning around, I find out who the white outfit belongs to. It's the rude blonde girl from the party. Her skirt is white, tight, the hemline way above her knees. The shirt she's wearing is also white, with big black polka dots.

Gemma continues to glare at her. "That has got to be a fake tan. And button up your shirt, chica. This is a funeral not a stripclub."

The rude blonde girl approaches and slides into the pew directly behind us, along with some woman, probably her mother.

Gemma grumbles. "I don't know what Bridger sees in her.

She looks so trashy and cheap. Did you see her blue eyeshadow? If she thinks she's being retro, she is sadly mistaken."

There's a tap on my shoulder. I slowly turn around.

The rude blonde girl smiles at me, revealing the braces on her teeth. "I wanted to apologize for what happened at Bridger's party," she says. "I was on the verge of peeing my pants and really needed to use the bathroom. You can understand, right?" She tilts her head. "I think I called you insensitive or something like that. I didn't mean it."

Don't lie, I want to tell her. She knows she meant it. And did she forget how she purposely body-checked me -- plowed right into me with her shoulder? Is she going to mention that? "Why didn't you use Bridger's bathroom, if you had to pee so bad?" I ask.

"Well--um . . ." she stammers. "Because I didn't think you would take so long. And I was the first one in line. . . ."

I shrug and turn back around to face the front. Whatever. She could have found another bathroom if she had to pee that bad.

Gemma leans in, grinning. "Do you know how happy I am right now?"

Did I miss something? "Why?"

"I think she doesn't know where Bridger's bedroom is. Which means things must not be very serious between them."

"Oh. Yeah, probably not."

The noise level suddenly plunges. Bellany's family is entering the chapel. Bridger has on a pair of dark sunglasses and is wearing a black suit. His father is next to him, also in a black suit, minus the sunglasses. There's no mother present. Wow. She didn't even come to her own daughter's funeral. Is that because Bellany ruined her life, drove her bat crazy and basically ran her off? Maybe she hasn't forgiven her daughter, yet. I can't imagine what she must be feeling. Are the memories just too painful to face?

Or, what if she can't come because she's living in an institution again and is unable to function in the real world.

Dang. That would be tragic. I really wish Bridger would open up to me about his mom again. I have so many questions.

Mom really dodged a bullet by breaking up with Mr. Silverfield. I think Bellany would have eventually driven her crazy, too.

Bridger pushes his sunglasses up onto his nose and wraps his arm around an old lady with gray hair, who I'm guessing is his grandmother. Bridger has been really struggling this past week. Two days after Bellany died, he asked me to make him a batch of homemade snickerdoodle cookies. I was surprised he wanted me to come over since his sister had just been murdered. But despite my being nervous, I went to his house anyway, showed up on his doorstep with cookies in hand and a manufactured sad look on my face. When in reality, I was freaking out inside. I didn't know what to expect or if I could convince him I was sad. I wondered if I could fake empathy, when I felt nothing remotely close.

Bridger was upset, but he wasn't paralyzed with grief or unable to function. He said he thought he had already cried every single tear stored up inside his body and had nothing left. Mostly he was angry, determined to find the person who killed his sister. Which is understandable.

I helped him design flyers announcing a $50,000 reward to anyone who could provide information leading to the arrest of Bellany's murderer. At around ten that night, some of his out-of-state relatives arrived. That's when I went home and was finally able to relax.

He asked me to go over to his house the next day, too.

We continued to spend a lot of time together, which has gradually gotten easier. We've made hundreds of flyers and put up posters all around Smithfield, Selma, Clayton and the neighboring towns. Just yesterday, his family increased the reward money to $100,000. But there still hasn't been a break in the case -- not that I know of anyway.

I'm ripped from my thoughts when Quentin's tall body comes into view. He's the last one to enter the chapel. His chocolate brown hair looks like it has recently been cut short and his face is clean-shaven. As he slides into the pew next to his mother, the devastated look on his face becomes more noticeable.

Gemma leans in, grumbling under her breath. "I thought Quentin was going to sit with us. He's such a momma's boy!"

The empty seat next to me was reserved for him, just in case he didn't want to sit by his mom. But I'm not upset. I'm just glad he's here. I hope I'll get a chance to talk to him after the service and find out how he's doing.

As soon as everyone is seated, a pair of wing tipped shoes and navy blue slacks appear at my side. My eyes travel up the person hovering next to me. It's Ace. He's wearing a crisp, light blue, button up shirt, bow tie and suspenders -- not the grandpa kind of suspenders, the trendy kind. Does he seriously want to sit by me?

I scoot over a few more inches. Ace sits down. The bench creaks, even though he isn't a big guy and can't be that heavy. There's about four inches of space between him and I.

Does he remember what he said to me the night of the party when he was drunk? He asked me if I wanted to party with him. That was so bizarre. And now he's sitting next to me in front of tons of people from school.

From the corner of my eye, I see Ace's phone in his grasp. I wonder what kinds of things he has stored on it. Has he already posted all of his scandalous videos, or does he keep some to save for later? I wonder if he has ever blackmailed someone with one of his videos.

I still have the audio recording of Bellany's conversation with big G. When she stole my phone the night of the party, she wasn't able to access the content and erase it. My phone requires a four digit pin number to unlock it.

I fear that if anyone were to hear the recording, it would absolutely ruin me. The recording proves that I knew Bellany would be in the woods the night of her party. It's not too big of a leap to infer that I could be the one who murdered her, since

I knew where she was going and when she would be there. But even though the recording may possibly incriminate me, I can't bring myself to delete it. What if I end up needing it for some reason later?

The double doors at the front of the chapel open slowly. Two men wheel in a white casket. I look away and accidentally meet Ace's gaze. Was he staring at me?

"You look pale," he whispers, studying my face. "Are you okay?"

I nod in response. My eyes lower to my hands as I squeeze and twist the handkerchief. I feel hot and sweaty. But I'm not nauseous, thank goodness.

The minister starts to speak. I take the program from Gemma that she was using to fan herself with earlier and try it out for myself, hoping to cool down. In addition to my armpits sweating, now my hands feel clammy.

Memories from the woods the night Bellany was killed come flooding through my mind. The flashlight I had with me wasn't very bright, but I remember pointing it directly in Bellany's face. I could've sworn her lips looked blue, which I thought meant she was dead. Still, there's that little bit of doubt lingering in my mind -- maybe she was barely hanging on to life.

I fan myself more vigorously, feeling no relief. I'm thinking about the noise in the bushes and how it spooked me. Why would the wind make one single area of the woods shake so much harder than everywhere else around it? The wind wouldn't do that, unless there was a tornado or a whirlwind, but there wasn't a storm brewing. I doubt the commotion was caused by an animal. Animals are usually quiet, unless they've been startled.

So it had to have been a person.

Whoever it was most likely murdered Bellany. And they saw me. They know I left Bellany there and didn't tell anyone. They know I didn't try to revive her or call for an ambulance. What if they recorded me or took my picture as I was bent down over Bellany's body? I look up at Ace. Could he be the murderer?

I remember those scratches on his face. Were those defensive wounds from Bellany? This question still lingers in my mind.

CHAPTER 5

Ace is preoccupied with a game on his phone and doesn't notice me staring at him. No, I tell myself. He couldn't be the murderer. He doesn't have a motive. Those scratches on his face were probably from falling when he hopped over the fence, just like his friend said.

I begin to look around at all the people packed inside the chapel to see if anyone is watching me. Like Gemma said, Bellany's murderer might be here.

What does the "G" in big G stand for, I wonder. Do I know any boys with a first name that starts with G? Not that I can think of. Or what about last names? I don't know, nobody comes to mind. Maybe G stands for his middle name. Or it stands for a nickname like *gangster*. My eyes travel over to Ace again. Ace is a gangster, kind of.

Gemma sighs, drawing my attention. Her fingers skate across her phone. A split second later, my phone chimes. Loudly. My cheeks burn as I snatch my purse up off the floor and search for my phone. I fumble to enter the pin number, then turn the ringer off just in case it goes off again. Why didn't I remember to silence my phone? I can't believe I forgot.

"Sorry," Gemma whispers.

She's crazy if she thinks I'm going to read a text message from her when Ace and his wandering eyes are sitting right next to me.

I pick up the program to fan myself with it again, looking around for possible murder suspects. Behind me, I hear something muffled and squeaking.

Gemma mouths something with her full red lips, but I can't decipher what she's saying.

I turn to look over my shoulder, slightly at first. But curiosity gets the best of me, so I decide to fully commit and crane my neck. The noise is way too loud to ignore. It's coming from the rude blonde. She's crying. Really? Who is this girl and why is she so upset?

I face forward again just as Ace reaches his arm across the back of my shoulders to hand her a tissue.

The annoying crying continues.

"Drama queen," Gemma whispers. "She needs to stop."

I would expect members of Bellany's family to be inconsolable, or her besties from the cheer squad, but not some random girl who has a thing for Bridger.

When the minister finishes speaking, a dozen girls from the cheerleading squad make their way up to the front. Gemma's eyes narrow. If it were possible, I'm sure steam would be coming out of her ears right now. She hates all of them.

Gemma tried out for the squad last year and didn't make it, basically because she was sabotaged. She has real talent and is just as good as any of the other squad members -- I'm not just saying that because I'm her friend. Gemma took gymnastics when she was younger and can do a backflip. Nobody else on the squad can do a backflip. Plus, she's tiny and would be perfect as a flyer for stunts.

Both me and Gemma think that Bellany and some of the other squad members got a hold of the judging sheets and marked down her scores. Gemma said she knew they were up to something devious, because they were whispering all the time whenever she was around. So after attempting to eavesdrop multiple times during practice, she finally heard something that sounded suspicious. Bellany said that she had "brought the red sharpe." Gemma didn't know what that meant at first. But when the day of tryouts arrived, she discovered that the judges were using red sharpes on their score sheets. So why else would Bellany boast about having the same color of marker, other than to alter the judges' scores?

At the front of the chapel, the cheerleaders take way too long to arrange themselves behind the microphones and pass out sheet music. They all have the same forlorn expression on their faces and white ribbons pinned to their shirts in remembrance of Bellany.

The tallest girl in the center lifts her hand to give a signal, and they begin to sing a capella. I listen and cringe. This is terrible. They should stick to cheerleading and leave the singing to people who actually have some talent. Dogs would howl if they could hear this.

Gemma's shoulders begin to shake. I turn and look at her, wondering what's up. She places her hand over her mouth, eyes closed. Please don't tell me she's crying. I stare at Gemma, absolutely dumbfounded.

Her shaking suddenly stops, and she lowers her hand to her lap. I'm about to look away, but then I see a smile emerge on her face. She quickly covers her mouth again, and I realize that Gemma isn't crying. She's laughing!

I wish I could join her and laugh like I don't have a care in the world. What a huge stress release that would be! But I can't. I'm still trying to forget what Bellany's bloody face looked like -- trying to keep my emotions in check. The only goal I have right now is to make it through today without drawing unnecessary attention to myself.

The cheer squad finishes their song on an extremely ear-piercing high note. Gemma accidentally lets out a loud snort of laughter. An older man sitting in front of us turns and glares at her.

All of the cheerleaders, except for one, filter back into the pews. Some of them give Gemma dirty looks as they pass us. Gemma doesn't seem to care. She's still laughing.

The cheerleader behind the microphone unfolds a piece of paper to read off of it. I look down at the program, wondering how much longer this torture is going to last. She begins to shed a few fake tears between words. And yes, they really do seem fake. I'm a much more skeptical person than I used to be, all because I'd been manipulated and lied to by Bellany numerous times. She was an expert at it.

Last year, I found Bellany crying in the bathroom at school. I asked her what was wrong, and she told me that Bridger had driven their dad's brand new car and scratched the paint on the door. She said Bridger blamed the scratch on her, because he hadn't gotten his driver's license yet, like she had. He failed his driver's test. Then she went on to say that she got grounded and had to pay to get her dad's car fixed.

Gullible me, I believed her. It wasn't until months later that I realized she was lying about the whole thing. Bridger was showing me some pictures on his phone and we came across one of him and Bellany standing in front of the DMV sign the day they got their licenses. They were both holding up their papers with big smiles on their faces. Bridger did not fail his test like Bellany had claimed. It didn't take me but a half second to figure out why she had lied about the whole thing. Bellany wanted me to think he was a bad person so I would stay away from him.

The organ begins playing, and people start getting up. Finally! The funeral service is over!

Ace leans in. "How are you holding up?"

"Um. Fine," I say with a shrug.

He shakes his head, frowning. "This whole thing just blows my mind. I bet you miss her."

How honest should I be here? I don't want to go overboard with the lies, but I'm not sure where he stands exactly -- as far as his history with Bellany goes. For all I know, he could be big G.

"What about you?" I return his question with a question. "Do you miss her?"

He stares off, as if I have just asked him some kind of deep, philosophical question. His eyebrows shoot up. "I think the entire school is gonna miss her." He casts a glance over his shoulder. "Just look at all the people who showed up."

Gemma stands, waiting for us to move and let her through. She clears her throat. I know she's anxious to go talk to

Bridger.

Ace gets up, "Oh, excuse me," he says in a suave voice, all gentlemanlike. Gemma thanks him as she darts into the aisle, making a beeline to the front.

I reach down to pick up my purse, and when I turn around I run right into Ace's arms. He pulls me in for a hug. Do I look like I need to be consoled?

Ace lets go of me, seemingly unaware of how awkward that made me feel. "If you ever need someone to talk to, I'm here for you." He produces his phone, finger poised above it. "What's your number?"

I hesitate, again caught off guard. He wants my number? Well, okay. I hold out my hand. "I'll type it in for you."

Just as I'm handing his phone back to him, some random girl appears at his side. Thank goodness. I quickly scoot past him while he's distracted, wedging myself through the crowd, nearly getting stepped on by some lady wearing a faux fur coat and a big hat with feathers.

I'm about to pass by Wade when Gemma's words come rushing through my mind: "Who knows what you missed out on." Maybe I did miss out by not accepting a ride home from Wade. We've seen each other at school and during Spanish class, but we haven't talked since the night of the party.

I tap him on his shoulder. His deep blue eyes lock onto mine and I smile. "Hi."

"I'm still waiting for a replacement cupcake," he says with a straight face.

Is he joking? "Then why don't you go buy one?" I reply.

One eyebrow shoots up. "Is that how it works? You ruin my cupcake, and I have to buy another one? That doesn't sound fair."

"You could have still eaten it."

Wade nods, tugging on his tie. He hooks his finger in the collar of his shirt, pulling it away from his neck. "I did."

A laugh escapes my throat. I cover my mouth with my hand, realizing this isn't appropriate behavior for a funeral -- at least, not this particular funeral.

Wade seems amused at my reaction and finally cracks a smile. "Was that you laughing earlier, after that . . ." he pauses. "That song was sung?"

Oh gosh. If he thinks I was the one who laughed, then other people probably think that too. "No," I reply, wide-eyed, serious and slightly embarrassed.

He points at me, straight-faced again. "Then you were the one who forgot to silence your phone."

My mouth drops open in surprise. "Uh, um. . . ." As embarrassment rushes through me, I somehow manage to close the floodgates. Hold on. He's just teasing me. I need to lighten up. Mom has told me a thousand times that I need to learn to laugh at myself. Nobody's perfect. "Guilty," I say with a shrug and a smile. "But I wasn't the one crying. That was the girl behind me."

The corner of his mouth turns up, revealing a dimple in his cheek. "I would have preferred crying over what I had to deal with. See that lady over there?" He signals with his eyes to a slender woman holding a tiny brown therapy dog. "I don't know if it was the dog or the woman, but the potency of those farts. . . ." He points to his eyes. "The smell actually curled my eyelashes."

I start laughing again, hand over my mouth. "Stop making me laugh."

He puts his hands up as if to surrender. "Don't worry. I only act this way at funerals. They're just too serious for me. I hope I haven't offended you."

"Actually, I think I needed that. I haven't laughed in a long time . . . so thank you." As I glance to my right, I notice that the path leading to Bridger has cleared. "You heading this way?" I point.

He pulls his black neck tie, loosening it. "You go ahead. I'm about to get out of here."

"Oh. All right. Well, I'll see you around." I turn to leave, then swivel back to face him. I reach inside my purse and pull out my phone. "What's your phone number?" He begins to rattle off the numbers, and I hand him my phone. "Type it in for me."

Wade's fingers quickly skate across the screen. I tell him a quick goodbye again, then head towards the front of the chapel.

There's a line of people waiting to talk to Bridger. I consider going to Quentin instead, but he's surrounded by a swarm of girls, each one taking turns hugging him. The hugs linger for a long time.

The last person in front of me finally moves, and Bridger pulls me in for a big bear hug, squeezing the air out of my lungs. As we break apart, he takes hold of my hand. Most of his face is covered up by sunglasses and a dark, patchy, unkempt beard. "You are coming over to the house today, right?" his voice is low.

"Yes, I'll be there," I assure him. If I don't go, Mom will be furious, because I'm supposed to deliver a plant she bought for Bridger's dad. She didn't feel comfortable coming today, but she at least wanted to express her sympathies. The plant is in my Bronco, along with the snickerdoodle cookies I baked for Bridger.

"Good." He squeezes my hand. "The graveside service starts in an hour, so--" his voice cuts off before he finishes his sentence. His bottom lip quivers, and I realize he's on the verge of crying. "You could ride with me if you want to," he finally manages to say. "There's room in the limo."

He wants me to ride with him and his family? I can't! "But that's only for your family."

"Remember when my dad dated your mom and how I called you my sister? I still think of you that way. You are my family."

An overwhelming sense of guilt constricts my chest. I don't deserve to be considered part of his family. I left Bellany out in the woods when she might have still been alive. There's no way I can go with him. I've got to make up an excuse. "I-I told Gemma I would give her a ride." I make a face like I'm sad I can't go with him. "I promise I'll be there, though."

He nods. "I know you will. You've always been there for me." A single tear rolls down his cheek, and I feel like a knife is plunging into my soul. Pretending like I never saw Bellany's dead body is wearing me down. I'm withholding information from the cops that could possibly help with their investigation. I feel sick inside.

Just past Bridger's shoulder, I catch sight of the casket. It's only a few feet away from where we're standing. My heart begins beating fast, and I'm starting to feel nauseous, lightheaded. The image of Bellany's lifeless body comes to my mind. My gaze shifts to her portrait displayed next to the casket. I wish I could always remember her looking just like that -- healthy, whole, without any . . . blood.

When a group of people approach us, drawing Bridger's attention, I bolt for the nearest exit, passing Quentin on the way.

I quickly walk around to the back of the building to be by myself. I pace back and forth, attempting to clear my mind of unpleasant memories. How did I end up living in a nightmare? I never wanted this to happen.

"Hey," a small voice behind me calls and I jump.

CHAPTER 6

Turning around, I see Vivy sitting on the ground, her back pressed up against the building. She's wearing all black, again. Fiery red hair spills out from the hood of her coat that's drawn up over her head. She recently dyed it. Before it was all black. In her hand is a partially smoked cigarette. "Needed some fresh air, huh," she says. "Me too." A puff of smoke wafts into the air in front of her face.

I don't remember seeing Vivy inside the church. Her red hair would have drawn my attention. The color is quite bright.

She taps the end of her cigarette. Ash falls to the ground next to her combat boot. "I had to come and see if it was really true."

Vivy probably thought that Bellany would live forever and always be there to torment her. I guess I thought that, too. For some reason, bullies seem to have an immortal essence about them. Bellany was no exception. And people liked her, despite how badly she treated them.

Vivy stares off at nothing, hazel eyes lined with thick black eyeliner. "I wanted to see her lying in her casket, but it was shut." Vivy places the cigarette to her lips, hand trembling. "I arrived here super early. It was just me and the funeral guys. . . . I don't think that they saw me. I was standing behind all those big flower arrangements." She paused and swallowed hard. "Those funeral guys were muttering about something to each other. One of 'em got really red in the face. I couldn't hear what they were saying to each other, but clearly something was wrong. One of them walked over to the casket with some kind of long metal tool. He twisted out a screw from the end of the casket, then stuck the tool in the hole and started cranking it. They all crowded around, still muttering. . . . The casket lid only opened for a second, not very wide either. I almost gasped out loud."

No. She couldn't have--she can't be serious.

Vivy's eyes narrow as she shakes her head. "I don't know what kind of Houdini game her family is playing, but Bellany's body was not in there. That casket was empty."

What? "Yeah, right," I chuckle forcefully. Vivy's either joking, or she's delusional. Bellany's body has to be in there.

"I only wanted to see it, you know, to get closure." She puffs on her cigarette again. "My cousin died three months ago. I swear sometimes I still see him at random places, like at the store, or the movies, wherever. I think if I would have had a chance to see his dead body and touch it to make sure he was dead, I wouldn't have to wonder if maybe he's still out there somewhere. . . . People do fake their deaths, you know. That must be what Bellany did."

"Come on," I say, my voice tense. "You're joking. Bellany's body was in there." Quit messing with my head and knock it off. This isn't funny.

There's no sign of humor in her expression. If anything, she looks scared, like she has just seen a ghost. "I'm dead serious," she insists. "They opened that thing up and looked inside. Empty. I was about to text you to tell you."

My mind begins to swirl with possible explanations as to why Bellany's body would be missing from her casket. Maybe the coroner isn't done with her autopsy but her family had already scheduled the funeral, so they decided to go on ahead and hold the service anyway. Or maybe she was cremated. But then why would they have a casket?

Vivy smashes her cigarette onto the ground and blows out a final puff of smoke. She gets up, brushes the back of her pants off. "If Bellany faked her death and she's still alive, then something seriously shady is going on." Vivy starts walking away, but stops before she gets too far. "Are you going to ask

Bridger where her body is?"

How would I even bring that up? Should I tell him that there might have been a mix up somewhere because the casket isn't occupied? But then he would ask me how I know. What would I tell him? "I don't know."

"If you do ask him, don't tell him you heard it from me," she says as if she has been reading my mind.

"Right," I quickly agree. But I don't think I have a choice in the matter. How else am I going to explain to him how I found out?

"Text me and let me know what happens." She heads toward the street and doesn't look back.

There has got to be a logical explanation for Bellany's body to be missing. And the more I think about it, I keep coming to the same conclusion. This must have something to do with the autopsy. Nobody has been told how Bellany died, so maybe the coroner isn't done yet. I've got to talk to Bridger and find out what's going on, or maybe that's a bad idea. He's already so upset.

I race back to the front of the church, push through the double doors, and enter the foyer. Gemma is standing in front of the guest book. She sees me and points to the page. "Look. Principal Lang signed his name, *Principal* Lang." She rolls her eyes. "I swear, that man is so arrogant. He should have signed his first and last name, like every other normal person."

"I've got to talk to you about something."

"Okay." She runs her finger down the page, reading.

"Not here. Let's talk in private."

"What the--" she gasps, finger poised on the page. "Somebody signed in as Bellany Silverfield. I wonder who did this? This is hilarious!" she chuckles.

I examine the signature, not seeing the humor in it, but rather becoming more concerned. The fancy swooshes in the B and the S look similar to Bellany's signature. This is either a really good forgery, or Bellany wrote it. No, I tell myself. Quit thinking she's alive. That's impossible. Bellany is dead. "Come on, let's go down the hall."

We move far away from all the people congregated in the foyer and stand next to the drinking fountain.

I stare into her eyes, hand on my hip. "Did you write Bellany's name in that book?"

"Uh . . . no." She cocks her head to the side. "Did you?"

"Of course not."

"Well, I didn't do it, and why does it even matter who did? It's not like Bridger and his dad are ever going to look through those pages. Having a guest book is just something people do to make you think that they're grateful you showed up. It's all for appearances."

I glance around to make sure nobody is close enough to hear, then I tell her what Vivy said about the empty casket. Gemma is silent, still registering what I have just told her, so I continue. "Maybe Vivy is lying, but she seemed legit spooked about the whole thing."

"Holy crap!" Gemma whispers.

I go on to share with Gemma my theory that the autopsy must still be going on and therefore has delayed the release of Bellany's body. Gemma's shoulders are cinched up toward her silver hoop earrings and haven't moved. She seems zoned out. "Did you hear me?" I ask.

"You don't think that maybe she could still be alive, do you?"

I'm relieved Gemma is bringing this up, so I don't have to. "I think it's possible."

"I could totally see Bellany faking her death. She always lied, and she was good at it." Gemma brings her fingers to her mouth, chewing on her fingernails. "But why? Why would she fake her death? The only thing I can come up with is that maybe she witnessed a crime and had to go into the witness protection program. But that stuff only happens in movies." She pauses. "I wonder if her dad or Bridger know that she's alive. Could they be involved in this ruse?"

"Bridger wouldn't lie about his sister's death."

"Maybe her dad knows."

Gemma and I could stand here and speculate for hours about what might be going on, but that wouldn't prove anything. We need evidence. "I think we should go talk to Bridger and ask him if it's true and if he knows anything about it."

"I think Bridger already left."

Why would Bridger leave when the church is full of people? "Let's go see if we can find him."

We're about to pass through the foyer, when Gemma's attention is drawn to something outside. She waves me over. "Look!" She's staring through the window.

From the corner of my eye, I see something big moving down the sidewalk. The blood immediately drains from my face. Two men are wheeling Bellany's casket towards the hearse. For some reason Bridger is getting into his car instead of the limo with the rest of his family.

CHAPTER 7

When I arrive at the cemetery, I have to park far away from the grave site because of all the cars. Gemma drove separately, since I forgot to bring the snickerdoodle cookies and had to drive all the way back home to get them.

I shut my car door and straighten my skirt. My high heels sink into the dirt as I walk, slowing me down. When I finally get there, I slip in next to Gemma. She saved me a seat.

The minister invites Bellany's aunt to come forward and share a few words. As she begins to speak, I realize I'm actually kind of glad I missed some of this. Hearing people talk about Bellany in a positive light is beyond irritating. She fooled so many people.

I used to think that Mr. Silverfield was manipulated by her too, since he always took his daughter's side and not Mom's. But the more time I spent at their house, the more I saw what was really going on. Mr. Silverfield lost his temper, a lot. He would yell at Bridger and Bellany for the stupidest things. *Who drank the last of the milk? Who left the garage door open? Who moved the TV remote?* I realized, once again, that Mom dodged a bullet. I wouldn't want him to be my stepfather.

When I accidentally let it slip that Quentin's mom had murdered her husband, Mr. Silverfield ordered Bellany to go to the kitchen so he could "talk" to her. That's when he absolutely lost his mind. I was in the family room with Bridger and heard the entire blow up.

He yelled, slammed cupboard doors, threw things. I think he even slapped her -- I heard the noise. He told Bellany that if he ever caught her with Quentin again, there would be dire consequences. He threatened to take away her phone, her car, her driver's license, he wouldn't pay for her college education, the list went on for a while. Then suddenly she screamed like she was in pain. I asked Bridger if he should go in there and help her. Bridger shook his head and shot me a scared look.

I sat there listening in absolute shock as the screaming continued for at least a full minute. Then Mr. Silverfield yelled, "Our family has a reputation to uphold. If I'm going to run for senate next term, I can't have my daughter dating the son of a convicted murderer. You are to end it with Quentin. Now!"

When Bellany walked out of the kitchen, her eyes red, tears flowing, she looked at me with such seething hatred, I seriously thought she might come charging at me and plunge a knife into my chest.

The next day at school, I thought she would break up with Quentin, but she didn't. And I don't think it was because she loved Quentin and couldn't live without him. There were several times when I had observed her flirting with other guys. Plus, I had heard her talking to big G, so she was cheating on him. I think she went against her father's wishes because it's just in her nature to be defiant.

My thoughts are interrupted when a man in front of me stands. He looks a lot like Mr. Silverfield, except he has less hair. When he starts to speak, I learn that he is Bellany's uncle. He gestures to her portrait. "Bellany was always such a joy to have around," he says. "She had a love for animals and often helped me at my veterinary practice. . . ."

Gemma looks at me, a scowl on her face. I know exactly what she's thinking. Bellany was no pet lover. She killed Gemma's cat, ran it over with her car. Gemma's neighbor saw the whole thing happen and swore that Bellany was just sitting there in her car waiting for the cat to cross the road. Bellany claimed the cat darted out in front of her. Liar.

My eyes travel over to the white casket covered with lilies. I'm no longer troubled to look at it. What I want most is to get access to it. I wonder if there's any way I could convince the men in charge of burying it to open it for me. What could I say to convince them? It would have to be a very compelling reason. . . . Or maybe I should just tell them the truth. I'm sure they wouldn't want to bury an empty casket and possibly be held responsible later.

My focus shifts to Quentin. What would he think if he were to find out Bellany's body is missing? Would that give him hope that she might still be alive? Would that make him happy, or would he be angry because he'd been lied to? He's already been through so much. I have no idea how he would handle the news.

Quentin's eyes pass over me as he scans the crowd. His face is blank, showing no emotion. Even though we're sitting relatively close to each other, it feels like he's a million miles away. Hopefully he'll be able to pull through his grief, and soon, since basketball season is underway. I wonder if he'll be able to keep his head in the game when he plays -- *if* he plays.

His gaze sweeps back over the crowd again. This time he pauses for a moment, staring at me. He seems lost, lonely -- that's the expression I'm finally able to read on his face. I wish he knew he didn't have to feel this way. He's not alone. I'm here. Just like I've always been.

Immediately after the graveside service ends, Quentin heads straight to his car. I can't help but wonder if he's avoiding me. But why? What have I done? Has he forgotten that we're close friends? I was the one who helped him look for Bellany at the party. That has to count for something.

Gemma and I are still sitting in our seats. She's texting on her phone, while I watch Quentin's blue Camaro disappear in the distance.

"Don't worry," she says casually, eyes glued to her phone. "He'll come around and be back to his usual self soon."

"What did he say to you at the church?" I ask, wondering if maybe he said anything about me. Had he mentioned the card we dropped off, or the brownies I made for him? What about the text messages I had sent, or the unanswered phone calls?

"I guess to sum it up, he plans on hunting down whoever murdered Bellany. He's furious. I'm worried he might do something stupid, like kill the person." She shrugs, and her eyes lower to the ground. Her high heels have a layer of dust on them from the dirt road, the same dust is on mine. "I told him he shouldn't throw his life away. Because that's exactly what will happen if he tries to seek revenge."

"Do you think he listened to your advice?"

"Who knows."

I lean in. "But let's not forget. Bellany might not even be dead."

Gemma nods in agreement as people scatter in different directions around us. She taps her phone and pulls up a photo of her cat. "Bellany killed him."

I guess I should have predicted Gemma would bring this up, thanks to Bellany's veterinarian uncle who mentioned how much she loved animals. Gemma folds her arms across her stomach. "Whiskers always cuddled with me at night. Sometimes he'd get under the covers if it was cold." Gemma continues to scroll through the photos of Whiskers, telling stories about him, the same stories I've heard many times before.

When Bellany ran Whiskers over with her car, I thought Gemma was going to lose her mind. She was practically inconsolable. I had never seen her so upset. The words, "I'm gonna kill her," came flying out of Gemma's mouth over and over again. I had to take her car key away so that she wouldn't go after Bellany.

This wasn't the only time Gemma threatened to kill Bellany. The other incident happened over the summer, during a pool party at the Silverfield's house. Somehow Bellany dumped some red liquid right next to the spot where Gemma was sitting. Then Bellany squealed in disgust, loud enough to catch everybody's attention. The red liquid looked like blood -- menstrual cycle blood. What made it even worse was that when Gemma stood up, some of it was on her swimsuit bottoms, which happened to be white.

Nobody actually saw Bellany plant the fake blood, so we don't really have proof it was her. But it doesn't take a genius to figure out she did it. Bellany was the only person mean enough there who would do something like that.

The crowd around us has thinned out quite a bit now, and I think that Gemma and I are the only non family members here. I decide it's time to interrupt Gemma's stories about Whiskers. I nudge her with my elbow. She blinks in confusion like she's coming out of some kind of trance.

"You ready to go talk to Bridger?" I ask her.

"Oh, yeah. Sure. One sec." She checks her makeup in her compact mirror first and applies some more lipstick.

Bridger gives us both hugs. Gemma holds onto him much longer than I did. Once he pulls away from her, he straightens out his suit coat and tugs his sleeves back down over his wrists. "Where did Quentin go?" he asks, his attention is only on me. I'm the one who usually knows what Quentin's up to, not Gemma.

"I don't know. I haven't had a chance to talk to him."

Gemma shoves her hands in her coat pockets, bites her red lips. "I think he's just upset." She offers this excuse with a sympathetic half smile.

Bridger's face twitches into a frown. "I think he's hiding something. He's acting really strange. Do either of you know if Quentin and Bellany were fighting the night of the party?"

My entire body instantly becomes electrified and alert. This is the first time Bridger has brought up the possibility of Quentin being a suspect, at least to me anyway. "Why would you think they were fighting?"

"I don't know if they were, which is why I'm asking you two."

Gemma isn't answering him. She's quiet, which is unusual.

I shake my head. "I didn't hear about any fights between them. Quentin was really worried about her that night. He looked all over the house, and we looked for her out front. We checked every single car trying to find her."

Bridger scratches the side of his face, the tips of his fingers disappearing into his scruffy beard. "Why did he show up late to the party?" he asks. "Where was he? What was he doing?"

Gemma's pointy chin lifts, eyes widen. "He was at basketball practice. His mom had set it up months in advance and paid a bunch of money to get some hot shot coach to do a private lesson with him."

Really? Gemma hadn't mentioned anything to me about this special basketball practice. She usually tells me all about her conversations with Quentin.

Bridger cocks his head in interest. "I bet that caused a fight between him and my sister. Bellany never liked it when he put basketball ahead of her."

That's because she's a selfish, spoiled brat, I wish I could say. She had no right to interfere with Quentin's basketball career. Basketball is his life, his future.

"Bridger," I say, "you really can't jump to the conclusion that they were fighting, just because he had basketball practice. Quentin practiced basketball all the time. If they actually fought every time he practiced, then they would be fighting every day, and we both know that didn't happen."

Gemma props her hand on her hip, her skirt swaying. "Quentin had told Bellany way far in advance about the basketball practice he wouldn't be able to get out of. So to make up for it, he took her out the night before her party. He had some kind of special celebration planned."

He did? I wasn't aware of this. Why hadn't Gemma told me about this either? A private birthday celebration seems like a noteworthy thing for her to bring up.

"You both shouldn't be so quick to defend him." Bridger shakes his head, teeth clenched. "Bellany should have broken up with him like my father told her to. Quentin's the son of a murderer. He's unhinged, just like his mom."

I guess it's understandable for Bridger to suspect Bellany's boyfriend had something to do with her supposed death, disappearance, or whatever happened to her. Usually the perpetrator is the significant other, right? But Bridger's suspicions are really off-base. Quentin is a good guy.

"Since when did you start distrusting Quentin?" Gemma asks.

"Since when?" he repeats, voice sharp. "Since my sister was found dead on her birthday!"

Whether she's dead or not is still up for debate. I wonder how Bridger would react if I told him the casket might be empty.

"Did you ever find out how she died?" Gemma asks.

I think my jaw just hit the floor, I'm so stunned. I cannot believe she actually asked him that! I already told her he doesn't know.

Bridger lowers his head. I can't see his eyes behind those dark sunglasses, and now I can't see the rest of his face either. Is he going to cry? Is he going to yell? If I could see his eyes right now, my guess is they would be filling up with tears.

I place my hand on his arm. "You okay?" He's still silent. I raise an eyebrow, looking at Gemma, wondering if we should leave him alone.

Bridger slides his hands inside his pockets, takes a deep breath. "Because of the ongoing investigation and the autopsy," he says, his voice low, "which I found out could take at least six months to complete all the lab work, I don't know when I'm going to find out how she died. My dad thought he would know once they released her body for the burial, but they still haven't told him anything."

They released her body? Hmm. Okay. So my question has been answered. Bellany's body is supposed to be in her casket. It better be there.

CHAPTER 8

Gemma wraps her arm around Bridger to comfort him as tears begin to roll down his cheeks. The sound of his sobs wrench at my heartstrings. I don't want him to hurt like this.

Mr. Silverfield rushes in, coming from somewhere behind me. He pulls Bridger in for a hug. The three of them are huddled together, while I'm standing on the outside. I can't seem to move, though. My mind is buzzing with anticipation and determination. I have got to open up that casket.

Bridger's crying intensifies, drawing other family members' attention. They begin to swoop in, one by one, eventually pushing me and Gemma aside. This is getting awkward. Gemma and I aren't family. We should probably leave. I look at Gemma and nod. "You ready?"

"Yeah."

We both start down the dirt road. Gemma's yellow convertible is closest, so we climb inside and she turns on the heater to warm us up.

I'm looking at the white casket through the windshield. "I wonder how much longer everyone is gonna stay. We might be here for a while, but it'll be worth it. We've got to look inside that casket and see if she's in there."

Gemma adjusts the vent to make sure the warm air is pointed directly at her. She shivers. "I hate dead people. Do you know how hard it was for me to step foot in a cemetery? Let's just get out of here."

"Gemma, come on," I say, hoping she's not going to be difficult.

"You stay if you want to, but I'm not going anywhere near that coffin."

I look at her with pleading eyes; best friend to best friend. "You're really going to make me do this by myself?"

She holds out her hand, trembling fingers extended. "See this? I can't stop myself from shaking. I'm freezing cold, and I hate being around dead people at cemeteries. This place freaks me out. The only reason I came was so that I can be here for Bridger. I'm ready to leave right now. You can too. You don't have to stay."

"Yes I do. I've got to find out the truth."

"Well, good luck." She pulls the seatbelt across her lap, snapping it into place and grabs hold of the steering wheel.

Wow. I've never been kicked out of someone's car before. I step outside and turn around to face her, shocked that she's leaving me. I thought I could count on her, but I guess not. I shut the door, pushing it harder than I should. It slams loudly.

Gemma didn't tell me about the special basketball practice Quentin had the night of Bellany's party, which made him late. She didn't tell me about the special birthday celebration Quentin had with Bellany the night before her party, either. I guess there's no reason I should feel guilty about keeping my encounter with Bellany's bloody body a secret from her. We obviously aren't as close as I thought we were.

I get in my car and crank up the heater. It blows cold. Great. I consider turning it off and dealing with the temperature as it is, instead of waiting for this stupid old Bronco to warm up. Only, I have no idea how long I'm going to be sitting here before everybody leaves. Just get on with it people! Say your goodbyes already and go!

My Bronco is parked a good distance away from the gravesite, yet I can still pick out Bridger from the gathering of his family members. He's taller than his father, more stocky in build, and he has a full head of hair. The cluster of trees I'm parked behind has a clearing big enough for me to keep watch of everything that's going on, which makes this spot really convenient. Plus, there are other cars surrounding me here, which helps keep me hidden.

My frustration with Gemma fades as I continue to sit and watch Bridger. In my mind, I can hear him crying again. I can't imagine what he and Quentin must be feeling. If Bellany really is still alive, I don't see how they could ever forgive her for putting them through this.

I pick up my phone and when I swipe the screen, an idea pops into my mind. Maybe Wade can help me, since Gemma flaked out. Good thing I asked him for his number.

To my surprise, he agrees to meet me here. All I ask him to do is to "help me with something." He doesn't counter my request with questions, which is a relief. If he had asked what this was about, I wasn't going to offer him specific answers, because I know this whole thing sounds crazy.

Bridger's 1970, lowered Chevy pickup is parked behind the hearse. I didn't notice it sitting there until the limo drove off with his father and other family members inside. A few people still remain congregated around Bridger.

I feel a tinge of adrenaline pulse through my veins as I anticipate the task ahead. The answer to the burning question looming in my mind will soon be revealed, and I'll finally be able to know if Bellany's body is in her casket. I'm so pumped at the thought. As I continue to entertain this notion, more questions enter my mind: If she's not in her casket, and her body is not with the coroner or at the morgue, then where is it? If she's still alive, there must be some monumental reason for her to fake her death. What could that be? The possibilities seem endless.

Maybe she has been recruited by a special, covert government agency to be trained as a spy. Maybe she is in the witness protection program. Maybe she ran away with big G to live in some foreign country because big G is a mobster and has to go into hiding.

I sit up taller in my seat, watching as the last few people head to their vehicles and drive away, leaving only Bridger behind. He's sitting by himself, surrounded by empty chairs.

I pick up my phone to check for messages. There's nothing new from Wade. He said he would hurry, but that was twenty minutes ago.

A woman and her daughter cross in front of my Bronco, heading to another graveside service. Up ahead, a white sports car parks behind Bridger's truck, which is weird. The funeral is over.

I lean forward, eyes squinting to get a better look. The door of the car opens and a girl steps out. I'm not close enough to see her face clearly, but I recognize the white outfit and the hair. It's the rude blonde girl who sat behind me at the funeral, crying the entire time. What is she doing here? Why didn't she come earlier with everybody else?

She and Bridger embrace, and soon another figure approaches them, wearing a black coat with the hood drawn up. I don't know where this new person came from. As the person in black turns, I catch sight of long red hair and realize I'm looking at Vivy. What is she doing here? Why are the three of them together?

Even though I know I shouldn't feel this way, I can't help but feel left out, and not by Vivy, but by Bridger. I thought he and I were close. Sure, he has lots of guy friends he hangs out with, but I thought I ranked at the very top of his female friends. I'm the one he always turns to for help when he's in a bind, like when I came early to the party to help clean the house and decorate. I'm the one who has spent time with him nearly every day since Bellany died. I have baked him everything from cookies, cakes, to pumpkin bread. I have gone with him all over Johnston County putting up wanted posters, handing out fliers. What have Vivy and the rude blonde girl done? Nothing.

I haven't seen the rude blonde girl since the party, not one single time, until today. Vivy only shows up at Bridger's house around dinner time, like she's a stray cat seeking free food. She never helped with any of the flyer distribution.

If I could sneak up on them without being seen, I would. But the trees they are standing by are spread too far apart.

There's no place for me to hide. I groan in frustration, wishing I could hear what they're talking about.

Could it be possible that this *get together* has nothing to do with the funeral? Maybe it has something to do with Bellany's disappearance. What kinds of secrets do these three share?

Vivy was telling me the truth about the empty casket, right? Why would she lie?

My eye is drawn to the side mirror of my Bronco when something moves, and I catch sight of Wade's blond hair. He walks around and knocks on the passenger side window, leaning down to look in. I notice a black ring on his thumb, a leather band around his wrist. His shirt collar is turned up, black jacket unzipped. He's no longer wearing a suit and tie. He looks like he typically does; like someone who plays bass guitar in a band. I don't know why I think of him this way, nor do I know if he even plays a musical instrument. I motion for him to get in.

His steely blue eyes settle on mine, and I forget what I'm about to say to him.

"Did I make it in time?" he asks, slightly out of breath, pulling the door shut.

So I guess he was hurrying. "Yes, you're fine. Thanks for coming." I glance around the parking lot. "Where did you park? I didn't see you pull in."

"Through those trees." He nods in the direction behind me. "Out on the main road. You said to be discreet." He flashes a smile that seems a bit mischievous. "So what do you need help with?"

Here goes nothing. Either he's going to think I'm crazy or . . . no, he's going to think I'm crazy. I just need to blurt out what I have to say and get this over with. If he laughs, well, then he laughs. That just means we're not right for each other. He'll go his way, I'll go mine, and I'll try to forget that this ever happened.

"Over there." I look through the windshield, pointing with my eyes. "I'm waiting for them to leave . . ." I go on to explain what Vivy told me about the casket being empty and how I wonder if Bellany might still be alive. I talk fast so he can't interrupt. When I'm finally done explaining the situation, I stare at him, gritting my teeth. He hasn't laughed yet, so maybe that's a good sign. Or maybe it's building up in his throat.

"You think Bellany faked her death?" A slight smirk forms on his lips. His skeptical tone makes it clear that he doesn't believe me. But he hasn't started laughing yet, so that must mean there's still a chance I can convince him.

"I'm fully aware that this probably sounds ridiculous. I wouldn't blame you if you didn't want to help me."

His smile widens, but it's less mischievous now. "I've got to say, out of the realm of possibilities I considered as to why you wanted me to come here. . . ." he shakes his head, eyebrows raised. "This is not one of them. I thought maybe you were into some kind of kinky, weird stuff since this is a cemetary."

"Oh." My cheeks feel flush. Did he think I wanted to be with him? At the cemetery? I'm so embarrassed, and I know I shouldn't be. After all, he did show up. So that must mean -- no! It means nothing. He's not interested in me. I need to focus and not think about . . . *that*.

I shift in my seat, trying to act casual. I'm not even going to acknowledge what he was implying. Stick to the subject, I tell myself. Act cool. "No, I need your help with this whole missing person thing," I say all businesslike. "If it was anyone else who had died, other than Bellany, I don't think I would have this doubt. But this is Bellany we're talking about. My experience with her has always been that if there was ever any drama, scandal, rumor or gossip, nine times out of ten, the source of it could be traced back to her. Besides that, she's kind of psycho."

Wade brings his hands together in front of his mouth, fingertips touching as he considers my explanation. The ring on his left index finger is silver with a skull and crossbones imprint. "What kind of scandals are you talking about?"

"There was a rumor last year that a student was having an affair with her teacher. Mr. Flannery taught English Lit and happened to be Bellany's teacher. When Bellany got her report card at the end of the semester, she commented about getting an A in his class and said that she didn't have to do any work or show up for the tests. And whenever Bellany skipped classes and got caught, she would pull out a note signed by Mr. Flannery that excused her."

Wade's eyebrows rise. "Bellany had an affair with her teacher?"

I shake my head. "No. I think she was blackmailing her teacher, threatening to expose his affair. She started showing up to school day after day wearing lots of new clothes. And she mentioned something about how it pays to be in the right place at the right time."

"Hmm," he nods. "That is scandalous."

I'm not sure if I've convinced him that Bellany is capable of doing something so outrageous as faking her own death, but there's probably not enough time for me to tell him any more stories right now.

His eyes flick toward Bridger and the girls. "So what's the deal with these three?"

I tell him who the rude blonde is and how odd it is that she and Vivy showed up after everybody left. "It's like they didn't want anybody to see them together."

"They don't usually hang out?"

"The first time I saw the rude blonde girl was at Bridger's party. She doesn't go to our school. Vivy just recently started hanging out with Bridger and me a few months ago. I really don't know her that well."

Wade's phone chimes in his pocket, but he doesn't check it. "So until now, you thought Vivy and the blonde were strangers."

"Right." I'm about to explain more but stop when I see two men in dark suits get out of the hearse. There's a truck approaching them with shovels and a wheelbarrow in the back.

CHAPTER 9

My fingers clamp down on the steering wheel as I watch the truck park. "They won't bury the casket until everybody leaves, right?"

"You would think," Wade replies, sounding unsure.

The truck door swings open. A man with silver hair gets out and walks over to the two men. Seconds later, the two men return to the hearse and drive away. The man from the truck approaches Bridger.

Wade reaches under his seat, pulls the lever and scoots it back, giving his long legs more room. "So you want to get access to the casket, and in order to do that, you need my help."

I can't be sure whether Wade is interested or not. His expression is hard to read. "Yes."

"Do you want me to open the casket while you divert that man's attention?" he asks, pointing.

"We'll need a tool to open it. So he has to open it for us."

Wade's eyes narrow like he's deep in thought. "Maybe we can break into it somehow."

"Uh, I guess. I don't know how hard it is to do something like that."

Wade's attention shifts to me, his expression curious. "Let's say we get the casket open. What if, and I mean, if . . . what if her body is in there. Are you prepared to possibly see Bellany's decomposing body?"

"Yes--I mean, no." How can I explain this? I can't tell him that I've already seen her all bloody and gross. Sure, she'll look way worse now, but still. I think I can handle it. "I'm not afraid to see a dead body."

He smiles wide like he's looking forward to experiencing an adrenaline rush. Or maybe he's impressed because I'm not afraid. Whatever it is that he's thinking, he seems pleased and eager. I'm so glad I asked him to help me do this. "Okay," he says. "If this gravedigger doesn't open the casket for us, we'll probably have to get rid of him somehow."

"Get rid of him? How are we going to do that?"

He brings his hand to his chin, gazing through the windshield. "I could steal his truck and draw him away that way, but I'll need to locate his keys. I'm not skilled at hotwiring."

I chuckle at the thought of Wade driving off in the gravedigger's truck. How absurd. He would never do that. He's got to be joking. Right? Or maybe he would. Maybe he is serious. "Um, I don't think I have enough bail money for you to do something like that. Let's just ask the gravedigger to open it. Help me think of something compelling to say to him to convince him that we absolutely have to open it up."

Wade slouches down into his seat, thinking. I'm trying to think of something too, but everything I come up with sounds lame. How are we going to do this? Maybe our only option will be to do something risky like steal a truck. Am I prepared to take such drastic steps, all for the purpose of finding out if Bellany's body is missing? I don't know why I'm so determined to discover the truth, but I am. I haven't felt this driven in a long time. I'm borderline obsessed. What is my problem?

Maybe I'm just like Vivy and want to see firsthand that Bellany's gone for good so that I won't feel like she's still sneaking around out there in the world causing me trouble. Because that's exactly what she would do. I just know she would. Seeing her bloody body in the woods that night just isn't enough proof to bring me peace. I've got to see with my own two eyes that she's in that casket about to be buried underground, locked inside tight forever.

Wade reaches forward and opens the glove compartment and it flings open, all kinds of stuff falling out. His eyes slide over to me. "How did you fit all this in such a tiny space?"

"I don't know," I say, embarrassed that he's seeing what a slob I am. We both start putting things back in. Why did he open this anyway? Was he looking for some gum? A breath mint?

Wade picks up a silver earring with turquoise stones. I had lost the match to it months ago and forgot it was in there.

I shoot him a curious look, wondering why he's so mesmerized by an earring. The sunlight reflects off of the stones, making it appear more valuable than it really is. I probably paid five dollars for the pair. "What?"

"This could be a momento that you," he points to me, "Bellany's cousin, wants to place in the casket to be buried with her. And in case you're wondering, I'm also her cousin -- and your brother."

"You're my brother?" I give him a questioning look. "Do you think we resemble each other or something?" I don't want him to think of me as his sister. Is that really how he sees me? The last thing I need right now is another guy friend.

Wade's alluring blue eyes scan over me from head to toe, like he's cataloguing all my features. And yes, I'm feeling uncomfortable about this. I did check my reflection in the mirror right before he got here, but I could've missed something like smeared mascara or lipstick. Heaven help me if there's something gross on my face like a crusty booger hanging out of my nose. I just wish he'd stop looking at me like that.

We don't resemble each other at all. He has blue eyes. My eyes are brown, and they're shaped differently, more round, bigger. His nose is straight and mine is turned up. His hair is way lighter than mine. "I don't think we'd pass for being siblings."

"You're right. We don't look alike. Which means we must have been adopted." He grins again with that mischievous smile of his.

I chuckle and shake my head. "Sure, we're adopted. Whatever. I do like your plan. I think it might work."

There's movement up ahead. My eyes lock onto Bridger and the two girls as they head toward their vehicles. Vivy gets in Bridger's truck and the rude blonde gets into her own car. I wonder if they're all going back to his house. That's where I should be going right now. I wonder if Bridger will even realize that I'm not there. Maybe he'll be too distracted by them.

My finger taps the steering wheel as my pulse speeds up, anticipating the task ahead. The gravedigger is hovering too close to the burial plot, making me nervous. "What if we don't get there in time?"

"I'll jump down into that hole if I have to," Wade says with conviction like it's a promise he'll stake his life on.

"But what if the guy doesn't let you?"

Wade lifts his arm and flexes his bicep, which is concealed by his jacket. I have no idea if he even has big biceps. "I think I can take him." He grins, teasingly.

I smile, trying to relax some, but I'm nervous. "You must work out."

Wade gestures with a head nod, his attention on the gravesite. "Time to roll."

The white sports car rounds the corner, following after Bridger's truck. My foot punches the gas, and I speed off down the road, then park behind the gravedigger's truck. Wade and I both jump out of the Bronco. I'm running now. The gravedigger is kneeling next to the casket as it slowly begins to descend into the ground.

"Wait!" I call, waving my arms frantically. "Stop!"

The casket freezes in place, and the gravedigger rises to his feet, his large body unfolding into a massive, towering figure. His biceps are as big around as his thighs. A teardrop tattoo is etched into his skin, directly under his right eye. There's more ink on the side of his face in some kind of a swirly pattern, reminding me of a snake. "What do you want?" he asks, his voice gruff and deep.

I hesitate. This man with all these tattoos on his face isn't going to care about some stupid earring and the emotional attachment associated with it. He doesn't want to hear any of that. I'm still searching for the right words to say, a new lie to tell, when his hand lowers to his side and my eye is drawn to something shiny attached to his belt. A knife!

Wade reaches to shake the man's hand, and I gulp. If only we had discussed a plan B, or a code word in lieu of "abort mission." I turn and stare at Wade, but he's not looking at me. He's not catching the signal I'm trying to give him with my eyes, and he's standing too far away for me to nudge him with my elbow.

"My name's Chuck Silverfield," Wade says.

Tattoo face grunts in response.

Wade gestures to me. "My sister, Anna, and I have just returned from a trip overseas. Our plane landed a couple hours ago and we came straight here from the airport, but unfortunately we weren't able to make it in time for our cousin's funeral service." He wraps his arm around my shoulder, which surprises me.

Tattoo face casts a glance at me, and I look away. He isn't going to believe us. I think all that's gonna happen is we're gonna make him mad. And I don't want to see what he does to people who make him mad. This guy is pure intimidation.

Wade's hand gently rubs my shoulder, sending a jolt of electricity up my back. "Our grandmother couldn't make the plane ride all the way from Russia," he continues. "Her health isn't what it used to be, so she asked us to place one of her earrings inside the casket with her granddaughter."

Wade's hand stops moving, fingers squeeze my shoulder, and I realize he's signaling me, so I hold up the earring as Wade continues. "It would mean so much to our grandmother if we could place this in the casket."

Don't stare at his knife, I tell myself repeatedly. Act casual.

Tattoo face grunts again. I try to read his expression, because deciphering his grunting is pretty much impossible. I don't speak caveman.

He raises a large, calloused hand and scratches the side of his face over the snake tattoos. The beds of his fingernails are caked with dirt. At least I hope that's dirt. "You want to do what?" he asks.

If I could bail and run, I would. But we're in too deep. I hold up the earring, letting it dangle from my fingers. "We want to place this in the casket with my cousin, Bellany Silverfield. That's her casket right there, behind you."

His dark eyes shift from me to Wade. "I don't know . . . that's not my call. You'll have to take it up with my boss."

Wow. I can't believe he's actually considering it and didn't tell us to get lost. Maybe there is hope. Maybe he will let us crack open that thing. But the decision has to be made now, by him. Nobody else is going to give us permission -- not his boss and definitely not Bellany's father. "Sir, please," I say, feeling desperation boiling up inside me.

Wade retracts his hand from my shoulder and pulls his phone from his pocket. "Can you hold off burying her until we get permission?" His finger hovers over his phone like he's about to dial. I suspect Wade's planning on having a two-way conversation with nobody. Does he really think this guy's gonna fall for that?

Tattoo face shakes his head. "Not my problem." He turns his back to us.

"Sir," my voice rises a little too loud. Where I'm getting my confidence from, I don't know. Maybe I'm just a desperate fool.

He turns around and crosses his arms over his enormous chest.

"Please. It will just take a minute, and then you can finish your job."

He stares at me, his dull eyes fixed on my face. I feel like I've lost. It's over. Bellany has won. Again.

Wade takes a step forward. "I think you know what it's like to lose a loved one," he says. "It leaves you with pain that doesn't ever seem to go away."

I think I might know why Wade just said that. A teardrop tattoo could signify the remembrance of someone who's died. Either that, or he got the tattoo while in prison to indicate that he murdered someone.

Tattoo face turns around, and I see what might be anger building in his eyes. They're no longer dull but seem to be coming alive. My entire body tenses. Is it time to run? Wade pulls me into his side again. I wonder if he's doing this to protect me.

Tattoo face grumbles as he scratches his grimy face. He points at us, narrowing his eyes. "You've got *one* minute."

My pulse speeds up again. Is he serious? He's going to let us look inside? I can't believe it! Wade's a genius! All it took was reminding tattoo face about losing a loved one. Holy crap! Who would've thought this big guy had a soft side?

My fingers slide inside my coat pocket, grabbing hold of my phone. I pull it out while the man's back is turned and tap the icon to start recording a video. I want shareable proof that Bellany's not in there.

Tattoo face retrieves a long tool from his toolbox then untwists a screw from the end of the casket. He places the tool inside the hole and starts cranking. My heart beats faster. I walk around to the other side, preparing myself for what I might see. It's either going to be Bellany's pale, colorless face or yards of untouched satin fabric. Am I really prepared to see here dead body?

The casket creaks as it pops open a couple inches. I hold my breath, camera at the ready.

"What are you doing?" tattoo face snaps. "You're recording this?"

Wade raises his hands in mock surrender, placing himself in front of me. "It's not what you think."

"I know exactly what this is!" The casket slams shut.

"Let me explain," Wade urges. "She's taking a video for our grandmother."

Thick sausage fingers clamp down on my wrist. My phone is ripped out of my hand. Wade shoves the guy, but he barely moves.

"Stop!" I shriek, jumping out of the way as fists begin to fly. My foot bangs against something, and I almost trip. Looking down, I see my phone lying on the ground next to a tool box.

There's a large wrench sitting inside it. I quickly snatch up my phone, then the wrench. It's not as good as a knife, but it's something. And it's heavy.

Wade and tattoo face are a jumbled blurr. I try to train my eyes on the man's silver hair but the color is too similar to Wade's, so I zero my focus in on their legs. Wade's wearing dark jeans. Tattoo face has on brown cargo pants.

I wait for the right moment . . . and swing. A loud crack fills the air. Tattoo face stops, turns. Wade lands a right hook square in his jaw. There's a crack. I'm not sure if it's the guy's jaw or Wade's knuckles that made that sound. I drop the wrench and take off running. I head straight for my Bronco, the sound of footsteps pounding behind me.

"Go! Keep going!" Wade shouts.

My chest heaves, heart thumping, as I jump inside my Bronco. Keys! I need my keys! My fingers dig around inside my coat pocket. I got it! Wade jumps in, locks the doors. There's another loud crack. Fractured lines spread across the windshield like a spider web. Tattoo face clutches the metal wrench in one hand, his knife in the other, a wild look on his face.

Wade grabs my arm, snapping me out of my shocked and frozen state. "Charlotte," he says in an amazingly calm voice. "It's time to drive."

My foot mashes on the gas and the engine roars to life. The Bronco takes off, tearing through the cemetery.

"Turn here," Wade points.

I make the turn at the last second and drive out onto the main road, accelerating as fast as the Bronco will go. I watch in the rearview mirror as the iron gates behind us grow smaller until they finally disappear. That was a total disaster. A huge mistake.

I look over at Wade and gasp at what I see. Blood is running down his face. I grab a handful of napkins and shove them into his chest. "Here. Are you okay?"

Wade looks at me from the corner of his eye, napkins pressed under his nose. "I'll live."

I'm not sure if his nose is broken. It doesn't look super swollen, yet. I wonder if he's been hurt anywhere else. "Did he stab you?"

"No, nothing that serious."

Thank goodness. "I'm so sorry. I should have been more discreet with my phone."

"So did you get a look inside it?" he asks, his voice sounding nasally from the napkins plugging his nose.

"No," I reply, feeling defeated. For some reason, fate is working against me, and I wish I knew why. "I'm so sorry," I say again. "When I first saw the gravedigger from a distance, he didn't look so huge. If I had known he was a former MMA fighter, cyborg or whatever he is, I wouldn't have even bothered. . . . I bet you wish you had never replied to my text message." My eyes remain on the road, guilt squeezing my chest. "This is all my fault."

"Yeah, it is."

I turn and look at him in surprise. Beneath the wad of blood-soaked napkins I see the corner of his mouth turn up into a slight smile. My eyes shift back to the road, and I take a deep breath. I'm so relieved he's not mad.

Wade flips down the visor, looks in the mirror.

"Is it broken?" I ask.

He pushes the visor back up and points to the cracked windshield. "Yes."

"I don't care about that. This Bronco is already a piece of junk. I care about you. We should go get you an ice pack or go to the doctor."

"Don't you have an open house to go to at Bridger's?" he asks. "That's what those cookies are for in your backseat, right?"

Not anymore. I don't want to intrude on Bridger's time with Vivy and the rude blonde girl. "I'm not going to the open house." My foot presses the brake pedal as we approach a red light. "You can have those cookies."

He glances back at them. "I prefer chocolate chip."

What? He doesn't want the cookies? I look directly at him,

trying to read his expression, wondering if he's joking.

Wade removes the saturated napkins from his nose, looking at the blood. "The light's green."

I drive through the intersection, unsure where we're going. Should I take him to my house? To his?

"My motorcycle is parked outside the cemetery. I need to go back and get it."

He wants to go back there? But I thought he was going to hang out with me for a while, and I would get him cleaned up. "How about we go to my house first and get some ice for your nose."

"I think the bleeding has stopped, and my nose isn't that swollen." Wade palms his hair back. The knuckles on his left hand are bleeding.

This is not how I wanted this day to end. Why does he want to leave? Doesn't he realize I can help him?

I make a U turn at the next light and drive back towards the cemetery, wishing he would change his mind. But I'm not going to beg him. He's probably in a lot of pain. That has to be it.

"Are you okay?" he asks.

"Me?" I blink in surprise. "Sure. I'm fine. Not a scratch on me."

"I mean are you *okay*? You seem troubled, like there's something else on your mind."

Well, we didn't get to look in the casket, so that's troubling. It's also troubling that Bellany might still be alive, and I don't know who's helping her. . . .

"What are you thinking about?" he asks. "You can tell me."

"It's nothing." I switch on the turn signal and merge into the next lane. "I'm just frustrated about how things turned out. And I feel bad because you got into a fight."

"There's something else bothering you."

Can he read my mind, or am I just that transparent?

A slow moving semi truck pulls into the lane in front of us. I slow down instead of going around it. "I have a lot of stuff bothering me," I admit. "But it would probably take all day to go over everything." Does he realize I'm inviting him to stay with me, again?

Wade turns slightly in his seat to face me. "Why was it so important for you to find out if Bellany's body was in her casket?"

"Because . . ." I hesitate. I don't want to sound obsessed or mentally unstable. "I feel like I'm the only one who believes she is still alive. Well, except for Vivy. I don't know what her deal is and why she was meeting with Bridger and that girl. Gemma didn't want to stick around after the service to find out, so I don't think she really cares."

Wade stuffs the wad of blood-soaked napkins into his jacket pocket. "Why do *you* care so much about whether Bellany's still alive?"

No. I can't tell him about seeing Bellany lying there on the ground, not moving, and how I thought she was dead. I can't tell him about seeing her blood on my shoe. I can't tell him I'm afraid the police might arrest me for her supposed murder. I hate feeling like I'm never going to be freed from Bellany meddling in my life. She has already put me through so much, and I don't see it ever ending. "I'm afraid of what she might do." I bite my lip, wishing I hadn't said that. Wade's staring at me. He probably thinks I'm mental. I've got to change the subject. "What if we run into tattoo face again?"

"Tattoo face?" He smirks.

"Well, I don't know his name."

The cemetery is up ahead on the left. It's surrounded by a tall brick wall. The only way inside is through the main entrance. I'm never going to drive back through those iron gates again. My hands grip tightly onto the steering wheel. I keep my eyes on alert for tattoo face and his truck.

"Right here." Wade points to the side of the road at a shiny black motorcycle.

He has a motorcycle and a Charger? I pull off the road and park directly behind it.

Wade reaches for the door handle about to get out, then he

stops. "How did Bellany supposedly die?"

"Nobody's been told yet."

Wade doesn't respond or move for a few beats. "Hmm. Well, Anna. . . ." he says.

I look at him confused. Oh wait . . . the story he told tattoo face about us being brother and sister . . . he called me Anna. What did he say his name was? Oh yeah, I remember. "Yes, Chuck?"

There's a glint in his eye, and for some reason I feel like I have just leveled up in some private approval rating he must use to score girls. He raises his eyebrows. "Have fun at the open house."

Wait, what? I told him I wasn't going. I open my mouth to remind him, then I realize he hasn't forgotten. He thinks I should go. Is that why he's leaving? Would he have stayed otherwise?

"You can tell me more Bellany stories some other time. . . . Pick out some good ones," he says as he shuts the door.

Okay. So he does want to hang out with me again. I guess that's a good sign.

The back passenger door opens, startling me. Wade swipes a couple snickerdoodle cookies. "These better be good." The door slams.

A smile forms on my lips. Of course they're good. They're amazing. I baked them this morning so they're fresh. Which reminds me, I baked them for Bridger. Maybe Wade is right, and I should go to the open house.

Maybe I jumped to the wrong conclusion about Bridger. Maybe Vivy and the rude blonde girl just showed up to the graveside late. Bridger was probably lingering around so he could pay his last respects to his sister alone. He wasn't waiting for those girls so they could have some kind of a secret meeting together.

I flip down the visor to look at my reflection in the mirror and run my fingers through my hair. My focus shifts to the cracked windshield, prompting me to hit the lock button on the door. I better get out of here.

I merge the Bronco out onto the road, expecting Wade to speed past me on his motorcycle any second. As I drive past the iron gates, I look in the rearview mirror, confused at what I see. His motorcycle is still parked on the side of the road. But I don't see Wade anywhere. I crane my neck to look over my shoulder. Where is he? Something moves, high above the sidewalk near the trees. What? He's climbing over the brick wall!

CHAPTER 10

At the next traffic light I make U turn, head back to the cemetery, and park behind Wade's motorcycle.

Why didn't he tell me he was going back into the cemetery? Is he really daring enough -- or shall I say foolish -- to risk running into tattoo face again? I don't want him to get hurt any more than he already has. Tattoo face has a knife, doesn't he know that?

With my arms stretched overhead, I grab onto the top of the brick wall and begin to walk my feet up the side of it, high heels slipping and sliding as I go. My skirt hikes up over my knees as I sit on top of the wall. I look down at the other side, discovering a much deeper drop than I expect.

I toss my shoes over. My tights snag on the wall's rough surface as I lower myself down the other side. I hang by my hands for a moment before letting go. My feet land on a bed of pine straw, mixed with sticks and pinecones. I let out a groan in pain.

Tilting my head back, I look up at the wall, confirming what I already suspect. I'm not going to be able to climb back up on my own. I can't reach the top even if I jump. And there's nothing around here I can use to climb onto and give myself a boost. I brush the twigs and pine straw off the bottom of my feet, deciding not to put my shoes back on. They'll slow me down too much, and I might need to run.

The trees sway in the wind and a rush of cold air travels up my skirt, lifting it. I quickly smooth it back down. Great. No shoes, holes in my tights and now this!

Through a break in the trees, I discover I'm standing at the edge of the same parking lot I had parked at earlier. All of the spaces are occupied with cars. Another funeral service is taking place just over the hill. I can see the blue tent marking the spot and a few stragglers making their way there.

Where's Wade?

I hinge forward at the waist and run across the parking lot like I'm dodging gunfire. As I pass the last car, I slip behind a tree, ducking under the branches to hide. I'm about to move to the other side, but my feet freeze when I hear a loud vehicle approach. Looking over my shoulder, I catch sight of tattoo face's truck barreling down the road in my direction. Crap! Did he see me? I wedge myself deeper into the trees, heart racing.

A distant voice yells. I scan the horizon, wondering if it's Wade. Is he hurt? My stomach dips like I'm riding on an elevator that just dropped several stories. In the distance, I catch sight of tattoo face running after his truck, hurtling over headstones.

I didn't see who was behind the wheel, but I can only assume it was Wade since stealing the truck was part of his original plan. I can't believe he actually did it!

I sprint as fast as my legs will go, running towards Bellany's burial plot. Rocks dig into the bottom of my feet, but I keep going despite the pain.

When I arrive at the gaping hole in the ground, I hesitate. There's a mound of dirt piled on top of the casket. How long will it take to uncover? Will I get it done before tattoo face shows up?

And that's not my only problem. I've got to find that tool to open the casket. Luckily the tool box is still here. I start dumping things out and sifting through its contents, coming across lots of screwdrivers, but I don't see that special tool. I hope it's here, and I hope Wade is okay. What if tattoo face attacks him again, and this time he really gets hurt? Maybe he needs my help. Maybe I should go look for him.

My eyes flick up and my gaze is drawn, like a magnet to metal, directly to a single chair. There! Right on top of it! I see the tool I've been looking for and my heart skips a beat. Maybe fate is on my side. I race over to get it.

"Hey!" a deep voice calls. I spin around and see Wade sprinting at full speed. He flies through the air like he's about to straddle a runaway horse and lands in the pit, right on top of the mound of dirt. "Keep watch for him!" he calls as he starts digging with his hands.

"Okay." I quickly survey my surroundings. The road is clear, no sign of the truck or tattoo face.

Dirt spews upward like a volcano erupting. I edge my feet closer to the gaping hole, wondering if I should jump in and help. There's not enough time. We have to hurry! I take another look around. Everything's still clear, so I turn my attention back to Wade again, my heart hammering in my chest. How far away did Wade ditch the truck? Just how mad is tattoo face?

Over my right shoulder, something moves. My breath catches, eyes dart around searching. Is it him? Is he back? Then I see it move again. A bird. It's just a bird. I sigh in relief.

"Charlotte!" Wade calls. Half of the casket's white surface is showing through now.

"I can't believe it!" I gasp. "It's finally going to be opened! Here!" I say, handing him the tool.

I almost don't hear the other noise at first; I'm so focused on what Wade's doing. But something makes me turn around, a feeling in my gut. Then I hear the engine rumble. "He's here!"

Wade pries open the casket lid but only a couple inches. He strains to open it further. Nothing happens. It's stuck. He drops down to his stomach, peering inside. Can he even see in there? Is it too dark?

"You're dead!" tattoo face yells. He's running straight for us.

Fingers grab hold of my wrist. "Come on!" Wade pulls me along. I nearly trip and fall, but he catches me, and I quickly regain my balance. We run in the direction of the brick wall, and I'm already panicking, aware of the problem I'll soon be facing. How am I gonna get back up over that wall again? It's way too high, and I'm not tall enough to reach. I know we should go another direction, but there's no time to discuss this. Tattoo face is right behind us. I can hear his heavy breathing.

"I'm gonna slice you up!" he yells. And I believe him -- no doubt about it. I've got a crazy person on my tail who has probably already killed someone before.

Wade is slightly ahead of me. I know I'm slowing him down. He keeps glancing back to make sure I'm still with him. We pass through the parking lot, straight into the trees.

My feet tear through the pine straw. The muscles in my legs are on fire. My chest heaves as I try to suck in enough air to breathe. "Wade!" I gasp as the brick wall comes into view. "It's too high."

Behind me, tattoo face is getting closer. He's grunting like a charging bull.

Wade arrives at the wall first. "Step right here!" He laces his fingers together. I grab onto his shoulders, placing my foot in his hands, hoping this will work. My body is flung up into the air, stomach flutters. The coarse bricks dig into my hands, but I make it! I kick my legs over and let go, not even thinking about the drop on the other side. My feet land on the concrete sidewalk, and pain surges up through my shins. I'm falling again, off-balance, feeling disoriented. Then hands grab hold of my waist.

"Come on," Wade urges, steadying me and at the same time pushing me forward. "I'll be right behind you. Get in your car. Go. Get out of here!"

Overhead, I hear animal-like grunts. I run for my Bronco, not sure where Wade is anymore. I assume he's getting on his motorcycle -- at least I hope he is. The Bronco's engine cranks. I shift into gear, about to look around for Wade, but then I see tattoo face barreling straight toward me. My foot punches down on the gas and the Bronco surges forward. There's no time to check for oncoming traffic. I veer into the lane, almost closing my eyes out of fear of getting hit. Luckily the road is clear.

Wade's motorcycle revs, speeding past me, then slipping around in front. I follow close behind him for at least a mile, which isn't that far, but I already want him to pull over. I've got to find out what he saw!

We drive several more miles and end up in a neighborhood full of historic homes similar to Bridger's, only these are located downtown. Wade pulls into the driveway of a two story Colonial with a wrap around porch. Stained glass windows frame the oak front door. Wade's black Charger is parked out front on the street.

I'm out of my Bronco and up the driveway by the time he gets his helmet off. "What did you see?" I ask, breathless. "Was the casket empty?"

He sets his helmet down on the back of his motorcycle, blue eyes looking intently into mine. I lick my lips in anticipation. It's as if I can see the answer right on the tip of his tongue, but there's something else too. Concern? Confusion? He raises his eyebrows. "The casket was empty."

"Are you serious? You're not joking, are you?" I fire off my questions immediately.

"I wouldn't joke about that."

I can't believe it. Vivy was telling the truth. Bellany has done it again. She's played us all. "So she's not dead," I say, still trying to reconcile all this in my head. "She's still alive. She's out there somewhere. Still alive! We had a funeral for someone who's not dead!"

Wade stares at me, watching me pace back and forth. I keep repeating the same words, "She's alive." I don't want to believe it. But what other conclusion am I supposed to come to? Her body wasn't in her casket. I'm not even sure if she was dead when I found her in the woods. She has used fake blood before. She used it on Gemma at the pool that day at her house.

Wade catches my hand to stop me from pacing. "Hey," he says calmly. "Let's go sit on the porch."

CHAPTER 11

I follow Wade up the steps of the porch to the swing. The cushiony pillow behind my back wraps around my shoulders like it's hugging me, but it doesn't provide the kind of comfort I want. I want justice. I want Bellany's lies exposed. Where is she?

My mind is occupied with so many questions: Why did she fake her death? Who helped her? Was all that blood on her really fake? Why was she lying there as if she was dead? Who was she trying to trick? Me? Someone else?

Wade waits patiently for me to come back up for air after swimming deep in my thoughts. He swings us gently, not saying a word.

Maybe he can help me figure this out. Because I'm stumped. "Why wouldn't Bellany's body be in her casket? This doesn't make any sense."

"Good question. I wish I knew the answer." Wade leans forward, so he can look me in the eyes, and I notice the dirt on his face and in his hair, the blood on his shirt. "So what are we going to do now?"

The breeze in the air causes a slight chill to come over me. Proving Bellany's still alive is going to be impossible. "I don't know."

Wade stares down at the porch floorboards, then casts a sidelong glance at me from over his shoulder. "What happened to your shoes?"

Oh. My shoes. I forgot. And those were mom's shoes. I straighten my legs to look at my feet. The big toe on my right foot is poking out of a hole in my tights, and there's another hole over my knee. "I left them at the cemetery."

"Want to go back and get them?"

"What?"

He smiles, and I shove his shoulder.

The front door of the house swings open and a petite blonde woman walks out. The T-shirt she's wearing has a bunch of words printed on it, but I'm too busy looking at her face to read what it says. This must be Wade's mother. They have the same striking blue eyes. Wow. She's beautiful. Suddenly I'm feeling self-conscious, sitting here next to her son, looking like I just rolled down a hill, collecting a bunch of grass and dirt along the way.

She shrugs her purse back up onto her shoulder. Her head tilts slightly, eyes pour over me. Great. She's deciding right now whether I'm good enough to associate with her son. And since I look like a homeless person, there's no way she'll approve.

"Mom. This is Charlotte," Wade says. "Charlotte, this is my mom, Evelyn."

"Hi Charlotte." Evelyn smiles, and it seems genuine. I think. "It's really nice to meet you."

"It's nice to meet you too." I return the smile.

Her eyes travel over to Wade and suddenly go wide. "What's that on your shirt?" She points, just now noticing the blood.

"Nose bleed," he replies casually.

"That's a lot of blood."

Wade shrugs.

"Well, you're going to have to throw that shirt away. That stain won't come out." Her gaze shifts to me. I think she's staring at the holes in my tights. "I hate to rush off, but I have an appointment with a client in five minutes. You two be good," she says as she turns to leave. Instead of getting into one of the vehicles parked in the driveway, she heads down the sidewalk.

"Big Tony's Bail Bonds," I say, reading the words on her shirt. I've driven by that place several times before. It's located a block away from the courthouse. The sign out front used to read,

Bail Bonds For You. "Your Mom works there?"

"My stepdad, Gilbert, bought the business last May. That's why we moved here to Smithfield." Wade places his arm on the back of the swing.

"Your stepdad's name is Gilbert? So who's Tony?"

He rolls his eyes. "Tony is Gilbert's nickname."

That's weird. "Really?"

Wade tosses his hand up, shaking his head. "He thinks Tony sounds like a mobster's name. He says it's good for business and helps motivate his clients to show up for court."

The front door opens again and out walks a guy with a long, wispy beard that comes down to the center of his chest. He's also wearing a Big Tony's Bail Bonds T-shirt, but I doubt this guy is Wade's stepdad. He's way too young, probably only a couple years older than Wade. He approaches me with an outstretched hand. Tattoos cover his entire arm. "I'll introduce myself since this loser seems to have forgotten his manners. I'm Coop. What's your name?"

"Charlotte," I say, shaking his hand.

He looks me up and down appraisingly, which makes me feel uncomfortable. I cross my arms over my chest to cover up.

"So where do you know this loser from?" He gestures to Wade.

Should I even answer that question? He just called Wade a loser. Again.

Wade sits forward. "We were in the middle of a conversation, do you mind leaving us alone?" His sharp tone makes it clear that he's not asking Coop to leave. He's telling him to get lost.

Coop raises his eyebrows. "See what I told you?" he says to me, shaking his head. "No manners. Guess his momma didn't teach him right."

Wade jumps to his feet, right in Coop's face. They stand there, glaring at each other, not speaking. Please don't get into a fight, not again!

"I dare you," Coop taunts. "Go ahead. Hit me. See what

happens."

"You need to leave," Wade snaps.

Coop chuckles mockingly. "Looks like your nose already had a beating today." He grins and starts walking toward the porch steps. "I'd be careful if I were you, Charlotte," he says over his shoulder. "That boy has a temper. It doesn't take much to set him off."

Wade sits back down as Coop disappears down the sidewalk.

"Is he your brother?" I ask in disbelief, wondering if he acts like this all the time. How does Wade put up with him?

"Stepbrother," Wade corrects. "He's the only and favorite child of my stepdad."

"So what's his problem? Is he jealous of you or something?" I'm glad I wasn't cursed to have a sibling like that.

"He just got out of rehab, but I don't think it worked. I think he's dealing and using again." Wade inhales then blows the air out hard. The muscles in his jaw and neck still look tense.

So Coop is a criminal. "He works at the bail bonds business?" I ask. That seems beyond strange.

"Yeah," Wade replies, thick disdain in his voice. He palms his tousled hair back, eyes narrowed.

"So are you a bounty hunter?" I ask with a smile, trying to lighten the mood a bit.

But Wade still looks tense. My attempt at humor has obviously failed. "Gilbert and I don't get along. That place is off limits for me."

"Seriously?" He won't let Wade work there, but he lets his druggy son?

"Gilbert says he's kicking me out as soon as I graduate."

My eyes scan the huge, beautiful house, the stained glass windows and sprawling front porch. It's not like there isn't enough room. "Why is he kicking you out?"

"Like I said, we don't get along. Besides, I don't want to live here anyway." Wade sounds like he's speaking the truth. And I guess I don't blame him for wanting to leave.

"What does your mom think about your stepdad kicking you out?" Doesn't she stick up for her own son?

Wade checks his phone instead of answering my question. But I can take a hint. I have pried too much. Maybe he'll open up to me another time. I check my phone too. "I should get going. And you should probably put some ice on your nose." I'm not going to tell Wade that it's starting to swell. I'm sure he'll notice that when he looks in the mirror.

He touches his nose very gently. "If I had time, I would ice it. But I've gotta get ready for work."

"Where do you work?" I ask as I get up and head towards the steps.

"I deliver pizza for that Italian place on Market Street."

At the risk of making him late for work, before I leave I turn back around and tell him how much I appreciated his help today.

"Are you going to Bridger's?" he asks as I approach my Bronco.

I pause and stare down at my big toe sticking out of my tights. I'm a mess -- nowhere near presentable for an open house. I would have to go home to change my clothes, get some shoes, and fix myself up first. By the time I'd get there, probably only family would be left. And I'm not family. I'll never be part of Bridger's family. Maybe I could have been at one point. But I'm not. "No, I'm going home."

After I get in my car I look up at the porch, wondering if Wade's still there watching me. I exhale, disappointed. He's already gone inside.

As I'm driving home I see an advertisement on a billboard with a basketball player in the picture who reminds me of Quentin. I wonder how he will react when he finds out Bellany's body is missing. I'm sure he'll want to find out answers, just as badly as I do. Since it's still kind of early, I decide to go to Quentin's apartment and tell him the news in person. Hopefully I'll be able to convince his mom, Ruby, to let me in to see him, even if he doesn't want visitors.

CHAPTER 12

As I pull up to the apartment complex, I spot Quentin's blue Camaro and his Mom's rundown Toyota Corolla. She often borrows Quentin's car -- the car he saved up money to purchase on his own by working at the car wash and saving tip money since he was fourteen. His classic Camaro is close to being fully restored and far superior to her vehicle. While I don't blame her for wanting to drive it, it is his car and she should respect that. He bought it before she got out of prison, without any help from her.

Once in a while, Quentin complains about how his mom places way too much pressure on him to be perfect. He's worried that he won't measure up to her expectations. And honestly, he should be worried. His grades have been slipping and so has his number of points scored each basketball game. Ruby hounds him about how he needs to do better, try harder, practice more, stop being so lazy.

I've heard her say things to him like, *Remember Quentin, first you'll get a college scholarship, do a year in college, then you'll get picked up by the NBA. It's as simple as that. Yep, my boy is going to make me a rich woman one day.* Ruby lays it on thick like that all the time. I'm actually surprised Quentin doesn't complain about her more often. I wouldn't be able to handle a mom like that.

If Ruby answers the door, I won't mention anything about Bellany. Otherwise, she probably won't let me in, like the last time I came with Gemma. I bet Ruby never wants to hear Bellany's name again. She thought that Quentin had stopped seeing Bellany. I can only imagine how furious she was to learn that he had been sneaking around with her all this time, and even worse, now the cops think he might be involved in Bellany's supposed murder.

I want to know how Bellany fooled the cops. Did she have help from a corrupt cop? However she did it, I plan on finding out. But right now I can't focus on theories. I've got to focus on Ruby. I need to remind her that I'm nothing like Bellany. This should be easy if I bring up the subject of homework or basketball. Quentin probably hasn't done any practicing or a single homework assignment since Bellany faked her death.

Luckily my school backpack is still in the back of my Bronco. I run my fingers through my hair, put on some lip gloss, take off my tights and go barefoot up to the front door, backpack in hand. Quentin has a paper due in History this coming week. I'll be sure to mention this to Ruby.

I press the doorbell. As the chime sounds faintly in my ears, doubt begins to creep into my mind. Will Ruby think I'm being insensitive, showing up here the day of the funeral to do homework?

The door creaks open. Ruby stands there with her hair pulled back in a braid, tank top and yoga pants on, back to her usual self. She is obsessed with fitness. But despite constantly working out, she's still at least fifty pounds overweight. "Hi, Charlotte," she says, unenthusiastically.

I say hello to her, then begin explaining the reason for my visit, making it very clear that I'm here to help Quentin with his schoolwork. When I tell her about the assignment that's due, a worry line creases between her eyebrows. Next thing I know, she's ushering me into her apartment, offering me a drink and snacks before taking off down the hall to fetch Quentin from his bedroom. Wow. That was easier than I thought it would be.

I sit down at the dining room table and take out my notebook.

Ruby returns with a smile. "Charlotte, thank you so much for helping Quentin. You're such a doll." She straightens out the tablecloth, removes the vase of fake flowers and pads into the kitchen.

Quentin appears from the hallway, looking like he just crawled out of bed. The side of his hair is plastered against his head. He's wearing sweatpants and a T-shirt, his backpack in one hand. He doesn't say anything to me as he slumps down into the chair directly across from me.

Ruby sets down two bottles of water in front of us and a bag of chips. She pats his shoulder. "You're lucky you have a friend like Charlotte to keep you on track with your school work." She gives me another smile on her way out of the room.

Quentin's not looking at me, which is making me feel extremely uncomfortable. The last time we talked was the night Bellany died. And I get it. I understand that he's upset, but he doesn't have to act like this. Like I'm a nobody.

He exhales, leaning forward, elbows on the table. "You seriously didn't come here to do homework, did you?" He narrows his eyes, and I do the same to him. He has never looked at me this way before, and with his tone all snappy and harsh. I'm feeling a lot less sympathetic toward him right now.

"I didn't come here to do homework," I whisper. "This was the only way your mom would let me come in here and talk to you."

Quentin considers this for a moment. His shoulders lower slightly, face relaxes. Without speaking, he reaches down, grabs a notebook out of his backpack and drops it onto the table. The TV is on in the other room. I can hear his mom laughing at whatever she's watching.

He gets up and switches to the seat next to me. "If you came here to try to cheer me up, don't bother wasting your time." He flips through his notebook so roughly, I'm surprised the pages don't tear.

"I came to talk to you about something . . ." I hesitate. How am I going to say this? He'll think I'm insane. Who in their right mind would open up a dead person's casket? Only someone like Vivy would do that. Not me. I'm not like Vivy. I don't dress like I'm always on my way to a funeral. I'm not obsessed with death.

"What did you want to talk about?" he asks, sounding and looking disinterested. But I know that's about to change, real quick.

Ruby walks back in, tennis shoes on. "I'm heading to the store." She tugs on her coat, lacing her arms through the sleeves. "You two keep working. Feel free to order pizza if you want. There's money on the counter in the kitchen." She kisses the top of Quentin's head. "I'll be back later."

I shut my notebook as soon as she walks out the door. "Please don't flip out on me when I ask you this, okay?"

Quentin's dark eyes crinkle, mouth fixes into a frown.

"Do you know who identified Bellany's body?" I ask.

His eyes widen. I cringe, preparing myself for an angry outburst. But Quentin remains silent. The only noise comes from the clock on the wall. Tick, tick. "Her father did," he finally says, sounding annoyed. "Why would you even ask me such a bizarre and insensitive question? What is your problem?"

I swallow hard. Here goes nothing. Quentin's either going to kick me out or he's going to be a whole lot happier once he realizes that Bellany might still be alive. "This may sound crazy, but I'm not lying. Okay? I swear. This is all true. I'm not making it up. . . ." I go on to tell him everything that happened today, beginning with Vivy. She's the reason this whole thing started.

"Are you serious?" he asks with no fluctuation whatsoever in his voice and no signs of emotion on his face either.

"Yes. I saw Wade look inside the casket. He said it was empty."

Quentin is staring directly at my face like he's looking through me. I have no idea what he's thinking. Does he believe me? Is he mad? Does he hate me? Should I leave?

His chair flies backward. Adrenaline shoots through me as I flinch and lean away from him. I'm so shocked I can't speak. He sweeps his arm across the table, knocking everything onto the floor, then turns and kicks the wall with his bare foot. I scramble to move far away from him, my heart pounding in my chest. I didn't expect him to react like this. I thought he might be angry, but this is psycho. I have never seen him so angry before.

He grabs his phone, fingers tap across the screen.

"Who are you calling?" I ask.

Quentin turns his back to me, ignoring my question. "I need to talk to you!" he yells into the phone. "Right now!" He pauses as he listens to the other person on the line, which I assume must be Bridger. Who else would know what happened to Bellany's body? "You better get over here now, or I'll go over there, and I'll make a scene in front of your entire family. I don't care!" There's another pause. "I'll tell you what this is about when you get here! . . . I'm sick of you accusing me of killing her! I didn't do anything. . . . Where is her body? Why wasn't it in the casket?"

Quentin punches the wall and his fist goes right through. Holy crap! I gather my things, sling my backpack over my shoulder. A loud crash explodes behind me. Quentin's phone is on the floor, screen cracked. I take off out the door and run for my Bronco. My hand shakes as I fumble with the key. The engine sputters, then roars to life as I speed off down the road, heart pounding. I had no idea that Quentin had such a temper. He didn't have to destroy things. He didn't have to act like an animal!

I used to think he was practically perfect, except for his one blind spot when it came to Bellany. He had no idea that she was a monster. He refused to see it. Now that I've experienced this other side of Quentin, I'm wondering how I could've missed it. Does he blow up like this often? Or maybe he just finally reached his breaking point. Doesn't everybody have a limit, a certain threshold that once they go past, they lose all control? I continue to think about this possibility as I drive.

Eventually a sense of calm comes over me as my perspective shifts.

Growing up with a family situation like Quentin's would mess with anybody's head. Quentin was raised by his grandmother who was never home because she worked all the time. His parents had been removed from his life: his mom serving time in prison, his father dead. Quentin had told me that his father was abusive toward both him and his mom, which is why he found it easy to forgive his mom for what she had done. But still, having a murderer for a mother, an abusive dead dad, growing up basically on your own, and then add another tragedy to the mix, a girlfriend who supposedly gets murdered and you're a suspect . . . how does a person cope? I guess I shouldn't judge him for flipping out. He's been through way more than most people deal with in one lifetime.

My life isn't perfect, but for the most part it's pretty good. I don't have a boyfriend -- missing, dead or otherwise. My mom loves me and works hard to provide for us. When she's home, she's available and fun to be around. My father isn't dead, at least I don't think he is. But he is missing from my life. I don't know where he is or what he's doing. He took off when I was only two-years-old. I'm still reminded of him sometimes when I see the scarred skin on my stomach. He's the one to blame for my scars. I'm glad he's gone from our lives. Part of me hopes that he is dead and that he died a tragic, painful death.

I had thought that Bellany's death was tragic, possibly painful, but now I know better. She's not dead. I wonder what Quentin thinks. Does he believe she's alive? Does he think she betrayed him?

A couple more miles down the road, I pull into a gas station and park so I can call Gemma and tell her what happened. She picks up the phone on the first ring. "Where were you? Why didn't you go to Bridger's?"

She should know why I didn't go. She knew what I was doing. But whatever. I start explaining everything, and she keeps interrupting, saying "No way!" and asking me a bunch of questions. Finally I get to tell her about Quentin; how he flipped out, punched a hole in the wall and broke his phone.

"You should have called me!" she shrieks. "I would have gone with you to see Quentin. Why didn't you?"

Part of me wants to tell her that it's her fault I didn't call. She shouldn't have chickened out and left me at the cemetery.

She should have stayed. But I bite my lip and hold back that urge. What I really need right now is a friend to talk to, and I don't want to push her away. "I wasn't sure if his mom would even let me in to see him."

"Still, you should have called me, at least to tell me about the empty casket. I always tell *you* everything."

What a bunch of crap. *No you don't.*

"Hold on," she says. "Oh my lanta. Bridger is calling my other line."

What? "Put us on three-way."

She pauses. "Okay. I'll try." Her tone doesn't sound convincing.

The line clicks, and the call ends. Of course. I could've predicted this. I hit redial. It goes to voicemail. Thanks a lot, Gemma.

I get out of my Bronco and walk into the gas station's convenience store, phone in hand, hoping she'll call back soon. After all I've been through today, I'm desperate for something sweet. I pour myself a cup of hot chocolate and grab a pack of mini chocolate doughnuts. The cashier scans my items, giving me a dirty look. What's her problem?

"Next time wear shoes if you want to come in here," she says with her hand on her hip, loud enough for the entire store to hear.

I look down at my feet and my cheeks start to burn. I leave my receipt behind on the counter and head for the door, trying not to let the cashier's rudeness get to me.

I sit in my Bronco, sipping hot chocolate and eating doughnuts. My phone is on the dash, screen facing up. I'm dying to know what Bridger is saying to Gemma and what she's saying to him.

Why didn't Bridger bother to call me first? Why Gemma? Is he mad because I didn't come to the open house?

Quentin didn't tell Bridger about my part in discovering the empty casket. But Gemma certainly will, and I won't have a chance to explain or defend myself. I won't be able to tell him that I kept him out of the loop to protect him, or that I didn't want to put him through the emotional strain of waiting and wondering about his sister. I only did what I thought was best for him. Will Gemma even try to explain these things?

Gemma hasn't been able to go over to Bridger's house as much as I have, not since Bellany faked her death. She has had to babysit her younger sister while her parents work. Last Wednesday, she finally got a night off. That's when we stopped by Quentin's house to deliver brownies. Later that night while we were at Bridger's house, Gemma hung all over him, flirting with him hard. She kept touching him, hugging him, laying her head on his shoulder. All I kept thinking was, *what is your problem? The guy's sister was just murdered.* I got so sick of the way she was acting that I went home.

Before, whenever Bellany used to be around, I warned Gemma countless times to ease up on the flirting because it irritated her. Bellany would give us dirty looks and before long, she'd talk to Bridger in private, then he would make up some excuse so that we would have to leave his house. This made Gemma furious. More times than I can count, Gemma would talk about how nice it would be if Bellany wasn't around to interfere with her and Bridger anymore. Gemma almost sounded like she was sure it would happen one day. I guess she was right. Maybe she's psychic or something.

Last Wednesday, since Gemma's prediction had come true and Bellany wasn't around to disrupt her flirting, I ended up leaving by choice. Now I can understand -- in a small way -- Bellany's perspective. Watching Gemma throw herself at Bridger really does get annoying. Gemma sat so close to him on the couch, trying to console him, that I thought she was going to sit on his lap. She also purposely spilled soda on her shirt so that she could borrow one of his. She wore it to school the next day and made sure everybody knew who it belonged to.

Sometimes I wonder if Gemma's obsession with Bridger is a sign that she's not right in the head. Maybe she's crazy and a psychic. She brings up Bridger's name pretty much every time we talk. She texts him about a dozen times a day. Whenever we hang out together, if Bridger doesn't answer her call or texts, she insists that we drive by his house to see if he's home. If I ever tell her that I don't want to go, she'll get mad and act like a brat the rest of the time we're together. I wonder if she and Bridger will become an official couple, now that Bellany is missing.

I take the last sip of hot chocolate, noticing that there's a man sitting in a work truck parked next to me. He isn't going inside the convenience store. He's just sitting there watching me like a pervert, and I have no idea how long he's been there. Guess it's time to go.

I hope Mom's still up when I get home so we can spend some time together. If she's not, then I'll make sure to get up early and make breakfast in the morning. She's leaving to go on another business trip tomorrow, and I won't see her for a whole week.

CHAPTER 13

Mom is already in bed asleep, so I set my alarm for the morning.

As soon as I wake up, I check my phone. . . . Still nothing from Gemma. I send her another text but don't get a response. What is going on? This isn't like her to ignore me.

I keep my phone nearby as I make pancakes for breakfast. Mom is ready to go, her suitcase is packed and sitting by the front door. I think she's in a hurry.

I tell her about the funeral and the graveside service while we eat, but I leave out the stuff about Bellany's missing body. I'd rather not bring that up right now, not until I find out from Gemma what's going on.

After we eat, Mom has me drive her to the airport in Raleigh, which is about a forty-five minute drive. Usually she drives herself and leaves her car in long term parking, but today she asked if I would take her. I'm not sure why. Does she sense that I'm hiding something from her?

As we approach the exit on the freeway, she asks me about Mr. Silverfield, or Brad as she calls him. "So how was Brad?"

"He held himself together quite well actually." I wonder if that's because he knows his daughter really isn't dead.

"Oh good. . . . Did he like the plant I sent?"

I bite my lip and hesitate. Last night, I set the plant on some random person's car at the gas station and left it there. I didn't want Mom to see it and be disappointed because I didn't give it to him. "Yeah, I think so," I lie. "He was just really busy and distracted."

"Do you think I should have gone to the funeral?" she

asks, and I can tell this is really bothering her. Maybe that's why she wanted me to drive her to the airport.

Mr. Silverfield knew that Mom didn't like Bellany -- no doubt about it. I can't quote the exact words Mom had said to him, but she said something like, *We are done! Finished! And in case you don't know why, I'll tell you. It's because of your daughter. She is the most vicious, mean, and conniving person I have ever met.* Harsh, but true.

"I think you made the right decision not to go. There were so many people there anyway, Mr. Silverfield might not even realize you weren't there."

I pull the Bronco over to the side of the road and help Mom get her luggage out of the back. We say our goodbyes, then she heads into the airport. As I drive back towards the freeway, I pick up my phone and call Gemma. She better answer!

"Hello," she says, sounding all cheerful.

"Gemma, what did Bridger say? You never called me back." There's a chomping and crunching sound. Is she eating?

"I would have called you, but I went over to his house." She chomps again. "He wanted to show me the urn with Bellany's ashes inside. He insisted. He said he didn't want rumors to start going around school, so I should come and see it for myself."

"She was cremated?" I don't want to believe it. This can't be true.

"Yep." More chomping fills my ears. "She was cremated, because her mother is living in Europe and wanted half of the ashes sent there. The other half remains here with Mr. Silverfield. Bridger said the reason why they had a casket at the funeral was because Mr. Silverfield's mother would have had a heart attack if she had found out about the splitting up of Bellany's ashes. So that's why they did a big funeral with a closed casket. It was all for show."

My head is spinning. I feel numb all over. Could this actually be true? "So she . . . really is dead?" I ask in disbelief. Please tell me you're joking.

"Yep. Aren't you relieved? I know I am. Life is so much

better with Bellany not around."

Why didn't Gemma tell me this sooner? She could have at least texted me. I can't believe she didn't bother to call. "When were you going to tell me this earth shattering news?" I snap as anger builds inside me.

"I was about to call you when you called me," she replies, defensively.

"Why not sooner? This whole time I have been wondering where she is, what she's up to, why her dad lied--"

"Charlotte," she interrupts. "Don't forget that you didn't tell me about the empty casket until hours after you found out. And you didn't say a word about it to Vivy. She thinks you're intentionally leaving her out."

"What?" I gasp. "Vivy's the one who told me the casket was empty. She was the first to know. And I told you as soon as I could."

"No you didn't. I was third in line to find out. Bridger and Quentin knew before I did."

What does she want, an apology? I didn't do anything wrong. I glance down at the speedometer, just now realizing I'm driving fifteen over the speed limit.

"Listen," she says. "I don't want to argue. Let's just focus on the positive side of things. The witch is gone. She's probably rotting in outer darkness, right where she belongs. Let's just move on."

Fine. Whatever. I have plenty of other questions to ask her. "So how mad is Bridger? Does he hate me?"

Gemma laughs. "No, he doesn't hate you. I totally got your back. I told him you checked the casket, because you wanted so badly for his sister to still be alive. I made up some story about how you were afraid someone had kidnapped her."

I'm stunned and relieved. Wow. She lied for me. "So he understands why I didn't show up to his house yesterday?" I ask.

"Yep. I explained it all."

My fingers loosen on the steering wheel. I take a deep breath. I can't believe she took care of all that mess. "I was so worried he would hate me."

"Oh, I know. I told him that, too."

"You did?"

She chuckles. "Yep."

"What about Quentin? Does he know Bellany was cremated?"

"Vivy called him and talked to him. So he knows."

She called him? That's not possible. "But his phone is broken. He threw it against the wall."

"Oh, right. Vivy went over to his house to tell him. Sorry, brain fart."

I'm surprised Quentin's mom would let Vivy step foot in their apartment. Vivy dresses like death and her hair is fire engine red. Maybe Vivy went over there super late, like after midnight. That's when Ruby leaves for work.

"Here's the other piece of news I was going to tell you," she says. "Bridger and Quentin aren't speaking. Bridger is completely convinced that Quentin killed Bellany."

"But he was at basketball practice. He had an alibi."

"Bridger thinks he's lying."

I exit off the freeway to drive through McDonalds and get a Diet Coke while Gemma continues to tell me more about her conversation with Bridger. I'm sad that he and Quentin have become enemies, but I guess I can understand. Bridger wants someone to blame for what happened to his sister. He wants answers. He wants revenge.

I arrive at home and park my Bronco in the driveway next to Mom's SUV. The house is empty, lonely. Gemma's still on the phone. She's laughing at one of her own stupid jokes, which I don't think is the slightest bit funny. "Why are you so happy?" I ask her.

Gemma sighs heavily into the phone. "Because . . . Bellany is never ever going to mess with me, or you, or anybody else, ever again. Hold on." She pauses. "Hey, I gotta go. My Mom needs something."

The call ends and I toss my phone onto the couch, then lay

down next to it, my thoughts turning to Wade. I almost got him killed at the cemetery by tattoo face. And it was all for nothing. I roll over onto my side and grab my phone. I better call him and tell him about Bellany being cremated.

Thankfully Wade doesn't get upset when I tell him the news. It's not that I expected him to, I just feel bad for putting him through all that mess at the cemetery when it wasn't even necessary.

After the phone call, I eventually fall asleep on the couch while watching TV and wake up around noon the next day. I'm surprised I slept for so long. This was my first full night of consistent sleep since Bellany died.

I take a shower and spend my day catching up on everything I put off last week: homework, cleaning, laundry. All of those things got pushed aside, because Bridger monopolized my time. I'm surprised he hasn't sent me a single text today. Maybe he is mad at me, but he just didn't want to admit it to Gemma. Regardless, I'm kind of glad to get a break from him.

Wade sends me a text just as I'm about to make a sandwich for dinner. We end up texting back and forth the rest of the evening until about ten, right before I go to bed. Not once do either of us bring up Bellany. Instead, I find out that he can play the piano by ear, never had a single lesson. The only time I have ever played an instrument is when I was in fourth grade and I learned how to play "Hot Cross Buns" on the recorder.

Wade's most hated food is peas. Mine is black olives. His most loved food is sushi. Mine is chocolate. His stepdad, Gilbert, gets mad at him whenever he calls him Gilbert. He wants Wade to call him Tony. I reply with, "At least you don't have to call him big Tony." He laughs at that.

I'm about to mention how Mr. Silverfield could've become my stepdad, but then I decide not to. I don't want to bring up anything that has to do with Bellany.

I fall asleep almost immediately after we say goodnight to each other. And I'm wide awake again a couple hours later, which really bites. I just dreamed about Bellany being a zombie.

She was chasing me with a knife. It was the same knife tattoo face had. After experiencing that disturbing nightmare, falling back asleep is almost impossible. I toss and turn, count backwards from three-hundred, twice. Somehow I finally manage to fall asleep.

I wake up again the next morning to my alarm going off. When I grab my phone to silence it, I see a new text message from Gemma. She wants to know if I'm going to school today. I text back that I am. I roll over and bury my face in my pillow, feeling groggy. Maybe I should lay here for five more minutes. No. I better not. I don't want to be late for school.

After I get myself ready, I head down stairs to the kitchen. As I'm buttering a piece of toast, I realize that my thoughts have been entirely focused on Wade the entire morning. I'm wondering what it's like for him to live with a stepdad and stepbrother who hate him. Coop, called him a "loser" right in front of me. If Coop does that kind of stuff in front of people he doesn't know, I wonder what kind of stuff he does to Wade behind closed doors when it's just the two of them.

My phone rings. It's Mom.

"Hello," I answer.

"Charlotte," she says, her voice weary. I'm immediately on edge. Something's wrong. "A taxi just dropped me off. I'm in front of the house, and I'm about to come inside. I wanted to let you know, so I don't frighten you, okay?"

The front door opens a half second later. Mom's eyes look red. Has she been crying? "Why are you back home so soon?"

She hugs me instead of answering my question. "Come with me, and bring your coat and purse. I'll tell you what's going on after we get in the car."

I'm sitting in the SUV next to her feeling confused, concerned, and a little scared. She has never acted like this before.

The engine is running. Mom's just sitting there being quiet. She finally takes a deep breath, then clamps her eyes shut. "The cops are looking for the person who murdered

Bellany." She turns in her seat to face me, eyes filling with tears. "Apparently they have some new leads they're following up on." Her shoulders shake as she begins to cry silently. She wipes her eyes with a crumpled tissue and takes another deep breath to calm herself. "I'm sure you already know that they have set up an anonymous tip line...." I nod in response. "There have been calls from people claiming to have seen a white Bronco pulled over at the side of the road where Bellany's body was found."

Time seems to slow down as I process her words. My entire body feels disconnected, like I'm floating. "They think it was my Bronco?" I ask, my voice cracking.

With a tissue pressed to her nose and tears flowing, she nods. "The detectives in charge of the investigation want to talk to you today."

In my ears, I can no longer hear Mom crying. I only hear the pounding rhythm of my heart speeding up. The night of the party, someone drove my Bronco. I know they did, because when they returned it they parked it in the wrong spot. Whoever drove my Bronco must have murdered Bellany! I'm being framed for what they did!

CHAPTER 14

Mom has already hired me an attorney. His name is Mr. Thatcher. I'm inside his office instead of at school where I would normally be at this hour. Mom is in the waiting room, because Mr. Thatcher wants to speak to me alone. I told her the whole story about what happened the night of the party. It wasn't easy, but I didn't have a choice.

First thing Mr. Thatcher asks me is to explain what happened the night Bellany died. So for the second time this morning, I tell the tale. Mr. Thatcher sits in his chair listening intently with a stern look on his face. I have no idea if he believes me. The whole story sounds ridiculous as I hear myself repeat it. I'm telling him the truth. Bellany really did lock me in the basement. She really did have a phone conversation with someone she called big G. And she did go out to the woods to meet him. I didn't do anything to her. She was already bloody and beat up when I got there.

I eventually tell him the part about my Bronco, how it had been moved to a different parking spot. "So since my car was stolen," I continue, "I should be able to get out of facing any charges, right?" I desperately want him to agree with me, but at the same time I doubt he will. This is murder we're talking about.

Mr. Thatcher leans back. His enormous stomach points up in the air, and I try not to stare at it. "You don't have any proof it was stolen. You never called the cops to report it. All you have is your word." He narrows one eye at me. "The detectives will think you're lying. Without proof, no matter how I try to spin this story, I won't be able to convince anyone that your Bronco was stolen."

That's what I figured. Nobody will believe me. Even Quentin thought I was mistaken when I told him my Bronco had been parked in a different spot. Whoever took my Bronco did it so they could frame me for Bellany's murder. But I don't understand why they would target me. I thought the only enemy I had was Bellany.

Mr. Thatcher sits forward suddenly. "What you're going to tell the detectives is that you drove your Bronco to the Silverfield's house as soon as you got out of school. Your Bronco remained parked there until you drove home that night. Understand?" He points at me with his fat finger. "You were inside the house the entire night." He leans across the desk towards me. "You are never to mention a single word about seeing Bellany's dead body. Got it?"

Where did Mom find this guy? I can't believe he wants me to lie. Does he use this same tactic with all of his clients? My eyes travel over to the diploma hanging on the wall. He received his law degree from some weird college I have never heard of. Yet he appears to be successful. His office is decked out with top-of-the-line furniture. His clothing looks expensive and the diamond pinky ring he's wearing is way more impressive than most women's wedding rings.

"Yes, I got it," I force myself to say this, and I swear the words seem sour on my tongue. Am I really going to lie to the cops?

He rises to his feet. "All right. Let's go."

"What?" My fingers clamp down on the armrests of the chair. "That's it? We're not going to talk anymore? Isn't there more we need to discuss?"

Mr. Thatcher waddles over to the coat rack and pulls down a long, charcoal gray overcoat. "They're expecting us, we need to leave."

My stomach twists and turns. I think I'm going to be sick. "Are they going to arrest me?"

He pats his pant pockets, checking for his keys. "They want to ask you some questions." He turns to his desk and snaps his briefcase shut.

I'm not ready though, I want to tell him. And I'm not sure he is either. Does he really know what he's doing? Has he thought this through? Is he absolutely positive I should lie?

I try to keep control of my breathing and slow it down so I don't hyperventilate. Don't panic, I tell myself. It's going to be okay. This will be over quick. And then everything will be back to normal.

Mr. Thatcher picks up his phone, drops it into his pocket. "When we're with the detectives, it is critical that you only speak when I tell you to. They're going to try to trip you up, confuse you. They're going to make you feel like you've already been found guilty in a court of law." He points at me. "Don't fall for it! Trust me, I know what I'm doing."

Really? Is he absolutely positive he knows what he's doing? I feel like he's rushing through things so he can get on with his day. Is he afraid he'll miss lunch? Does he have a golf game to get to? My entire future is at stake here. Does he even care?

The door to his office swings open and he stands next to it, waiting for me to walk through, tapping his foot impatiently. I pry my fingers off the chair and force myself to stand. My legs feel shaky, even before I ride the elevator down to the parking garage. Mom has her arm around me, which helps me calm down a little. I'm so glad she was able to come back from her trip. There's no way I could do this without her.

Mr. Thatcher directs us to his completely decked out Tesla. Mom sits in the front passenger seat next to him. I'm in the back, my nose overpowered with the intoxicating new car smell.

During the drive to the police station, he informs Mom that it's best she not be present when the detectives question me, assuring her that he knows what he's doing. Mom seems hesitant to agree to this at first, but she eventually gives in to his request. I'm not so sure I like this idea. Again, I'm questioning his competency.

I don't know if he got rich because he's a good lawyer, or if it's because he's corrupt. Or what if this is all just a big facade. Maybe this Tesla isn't his. Maybe he rented it. And what about his office, is it even his? I didn't see his name on the door. What else could he be lying about? Is that diamond in his ring even real?

The ride to the police station goes by way too quickly. I'm not sure if time has sped up. It definitely feels like it has. I just wish this wasn't really happening. Why can't it all just be another nightmare? Why is life so unfair? What did I ever do to deserve this? Bad things aren't supposed to happen to good people. . . . My thoughts continue to scatter in every direction as we approach the main entrance of the police station.

Mr. Thatcher pauses before the doors open and turns to face me. For the first time, he smiles. But his smile looks fake, forced. "Do you need me to go over what you're supposed to say again?" he asks.

"No," I reply. I know what he wants me to say, only I'm just not sure I'm going to say it.

CHAPTER 15

The front door to the police station opens and as soon as we walk inside, my mind begins to fill with fog. I can barely think straight. My entire body feels shaky -- inside and out. It's not until I'm sitting in the interrogation room with Mr. Thatcher and two detectives, that I'm finally able to gain an ounce of control over my thoughts. I'm trying desperately to focus on what they're saying.

The detectives introduce themselves: The female's name is Detective Rodriguez, the male, Detective Monroe. They inform me that several eyewitnesses claim to have seen my Bronco parked at the side of the road the night Bellany was murdered, just fifty feet away from where her body was found.

I sit in my chair and listen, trying not to cry, trying to present myself like I'm an innocent person. Only I'm not sure what an innocent person is supposed to act like. I didn't kill Bellany, so in this aspect I am innocent. But I'm guilty of withholding information -- information that could possibly help in their investigation. Can they sense this about me? Do they know I'm hiding something?

If I decide to come clean and tell them everything that happened, I worry what the consequences might be. I had the means, motive, and opportunity to kill Bellany. I fear informing the detectives of these facts would only lead to my arrest.

A file folder lands on the table in front of Detective Rodriguez. When she flips it open, air fans upward. Her wispy bangs flutter in the breeze. A photo is slid across the table. "Charlotte, I want you to take a look at this picture. We received this in the mail yesterday." She taps it with her bony finger. "This white Bronco was parked alongside Highway two-ten, in close proximity to the location where Bellany's body was found."

My eyes remain glued to the picture as Mr. Thatcher leans in over my shoulder, examining the photo. "Yes, it is a white Bronco," he says.

The angle that the photo was taken makes it difficult to see who is sitting behind the wheel. But I recognize the smiley face bumper sticker on the back window and the dent on the rear fender. It's my Bronco.

Detective Rodriguez slides another photo in front of me. "Here is a close up of the license plate. The Bronco is registered to you, Charlotte."

My stomach sinks. They might as well go ahead and slap the cuffs on me right now. They have placed my vehicle at the scene of the crime. What more is there to prove? My attorney certainly isn't any help. He's an absolute idiot! He's just sitting here, letting them bury me with evidence.

Mr. Thatcher lowers his glasses to the edge of his long nose, leaning in closer to the photo. Do something besides stare at it, I want to scream at him. It's a photo of a license plate, not a Where's Waldo. Step up and act like an attorney!

"Charlotte," Detective Rodriguez says calmly. Her petite frame, narrow face and sunken in cheeks make her appear weak, yet her badge seems to make up for all of her physical frailties. "Did you kill Bellany?"

Mr. Thatcher looks at me and gives me a nod.

"No," I say, my voice barely above a whisper. Does she believe me?

Detective Rodriguez remains focused, her gaze steady. "What were you doing parked on the side of the road, Charlotte? What happened that night?"

Mr. Thatcher jams his fat finger down onto the table, looking Detective Rodriguez squarely in the eye. "This photo could have been taken on any night. It could have been doctored for all we know."

Her lips twist, just slightly. "This picture puts Charlotte's Bronco at the scene of the crime. Multiple eyewitnesses have also confirmed this." Her eyes settle on me again. "What were you doing parked on the side of the road?"

Mr. Thatcher scoots his chair out. Metal scrapes across the floor. "We're done here."

Before he gets up, Detective Monroe steps forward. His nostrils flare as he inhales. "She can answer the question *now,* or she can answer it in front of a judge. Which do you prefer?"

Mr. Thatcher and Detective Monroe argue back and forth while I continue to stare down at the photo. My vision's beginning to blur, not because of tears in my eyes, but because I forgot to blink. I don't want to believe this is happening, yet I can't deny the evidence staring right at me. This is absolutely crazy! Who sent this photo to the detectives? Who called? Someone is setting me up!

My pulse is racing, sweat beading on my forehead. Next to me, Mr. Thatcher is starting to repeat himself as he responds to Detective Monroe. It sounds like he's losing the argument, and I'm losing all hope.

I can't sit back any longer and let my lawyer make a mess of things. I've got to say something. "That's my Bronco," I blurt out. The room falls silent. "I stopped at the side of the road before the party, because my Bronco had a flat tire." The lie flies out of my mouth with such conviction, I almost believe it myself.

Detective Rodriguez scoots forward in her chair, folding her hands together. "Did anyone come and help you change your flat tire? Do you have anyone who can corroborate your story?"

Corroborate? Of course! Yes, that's a great idea. But who? Definitely not Gemma -- she'll cave under the pressure. Not Vivy -- she's not reputable enough. There's only one logical choice. "Wade Toben," I say. "He changed my tire for me. He was with me. We go to school together."

Detective Rodriguez picks up her pen and asks me to tell her exactly when this happened, how long I was parked there. . . . As she takes notes, Mr. Thatcher runs his mouth to Detective Monroe, acting like he has just laid down a winning hand of cards, when in reality he has done nothing.

I feel a sense of relief, but at the same time I'm freaking out inside. Is this enough to get them to leave me alone? Will they take me off the suspect list now?

The conversation going on around me is a bunch of jumbled words and might as well be spoken in a foreign language, until Mr. Thatcher chuckles, pulling me from the fog. I force myself to concentrate and listen. Why is he laughing?

Mr. Thatcher chuckles again. "They'll give anybody a detective badge these days," he says to Detective Monroe.

When Detective Monroe turns his stone cold gaze on me instead of responding to Mr. Thatcher's insult, I feel the blood drain from my face. He reaches inside his jacket pocket and pulls out a picture of Bellany. "You know, Charlotte . . . you look a lot like Bellany. You both have golden-brown hair, and it's the same length. She even styled it like you. Or did you copy her?" He pulls another photo. This one from the file folder. It's a picture of Bellany's car. "You both own the same type of vehicle. A Bronco. Only Bellany's Bronco is much newer and nicer than yours. . . . So many similarities. . . . They couldn't be coincidences, right? Wouldn't you agree?"

He thinks I copied her? Well, I didn't. My hair color is natural, and I've always worn it long. I style it like most other girls at school do, because this is a popular hairstyle, not because of Bellany. And so what if I drive the same type of car Bellany did.

Monroe sets another photo of Bellany down on the table. "Bellany was on the cheerleading squad. You tried out for cheerleading too, but you didn't make it. That must've been a real disappointment for you, maybe even humiliating. . . . Did it make you jealous to see Bellany in her cheerleading uniform cheering at ball games and at pep rallies, hanging out with the popular kids? She was in the limelight, while you had to sit on the bleachers and watch her get all the attention."

I cannot believe he's saying this crap. I wasn't jealous of her. I didn't get a chance to try out for the squad. On the third day of practice, I got dropped while doing a stunt and twisted my ankle, so I couldn't try out. I could barely walk.

Detective Monroe leans onto the table. The fluorescent light in here reflects off his oily face. "And what about Quentin?" he asks with a raised eyebrow. "I've heard from several sources that you liked Quentin, but he chose Bellany instead of you. Jealousy is a powerful emotion that can easily lead to hate, anger, rage . . . murder."

Who told him I liked Quentin? Maybe I used to like Quentin, but I don't anymore.

Detective Monroe pulls out a notepad from his pocket to read off of it. "I've heard from more than one source that there was a huge rivalry between you and Bellany. In the eighth grade, you both were on a school field trip when an incident occurred. Someone cut a chunk of your hair off while you were sleeping." Monroe's eyes flash up to me. "You blamed Bellany."

That's because she did it. She had scissors in her suitcase. I want to tell him this, but at the same time I'm not sure if I should. Maybe I should just keep my mouth shut, like Mr. Thatcher told me.

He looks down at his paper again. "There was another incident at school where the words *slut* and *whore* were written on your locker. You blamed Bellany for that, too." He pauses, takes a deep breath, then grins. "I have more notes to share, but we can save those for another time."

She wrote on my locker as payback for when I threw that cookie at her face. I know she did it -- the timing was evidence enough. I threw the cookie at her on a Saturday. My locker was defaced on Monday morning.

Mr. Thatcher lets out a raspy cough into his fist, then pats my shoulder. "Let's go."

I stand up, unsure if they're actually going to let me walk out of here. I keep my eyes glued to the back of Mr. Thatcher's suit coat, focusing on a piece of white lint. He's walking so slow. I wish he would hurry up. I've got to get out of here!

Detective Rodriguez comes to my side, holding out her card. "If you can think of anything that might help us find out what happened to Bellany, please give us a call."

I take the card from her, planning on tossing it into the trash later.

"Come on, dear." Mr. Thatcher reaches around my shoulder, leading me out of the room.

Our footsteps echo in the hallway, drawing Mom's attention. She rushes towards me. "How did everything go?"

"Just fine," Mr. Thatcher replies.

She hooks her arm in mine, falling in step with us. All I can think about is getting out of here as soon as possible. I've got to call Wade before the detectives do!

When we exit the building, I glance back over my shoulder. Both detectives are watching me, whispering to each other.

Mr. Thatcher begins explaining what happened to Mom, right here in the middle of the sidewalk. I take off towards the parking lot, distancing myself from them. I pull my phone from my pocket and dial Wade's number.

Please pick up! Please!

CHAPTER 16

The call goes to voicemail.

Looking at the clock on my phone, I realize it's lunch time at school. Maybe Wade's busy eating, or his phone is turned off.

I hit redial. The constant ringing drums in my ears.

Mom looks over her shoulder and just now notices I've left her side. I wave at her to signal I'm fine.

I hit redial again and watch a yellow leaf fall from a nearby tree, fluttering down to the ground. Before it lands, a breeze tosses it back up into the air. It bounces along in the wind helplessly, until it lands in the street, right in the path of the oncoming traffic.

"Hello?" Wade's voice finally comes through. My heart leaps in my chest.

"Wade! It's me, Charlotte. I've got to talk to you right now. Please don't hang up or ask me to call you back. This is important! I've really messed up and need your help."

"What's the matter?" he asks, the sound of his voice competing with the school's bustling cafeteria in the background.

He's going to hate me when I tell him what I've done. I'm the worst friend. He deserves so much better. As guilt and sorrow start to bind my tongue, he prompts me again. "What's going on?"

I open my mouth, forcing the words to come out. "I'm so sorry. I didn't know what else to do. I-I had to think of something to say--I didn't have a choice. They were going to arrest me for Bellany's murder." I hesitate again, feeling paralyzed by remorse. There is no justification for what I have done. He doesn't deserve to be dragged into my lies.

"Arrest you? Why?"

"People have called the tip line, claiming to have seen my Bronco parked where Bellany's body was found. Someone even sent the cops a picture of my Bronco to prove it. So I had to think of an excuse." The background noise disappears, and I wonder if he has hung up. "Hello? Wade? Are you there?"

"Yes, I'm here," he responds, his voice almost a whisper. "Hold on a second."

"No, wait! Wade!" There's no response. "Wade? Wade?" I check the screen. The call is still connected.

"Okay," his voice finally comes back. "How did the police get a photo of your Bronco? Who sent it?"

"I don't know."

"Hold on," Wade says. There's another pause. "The Smithfield police department is calling on my other line."

"Already?" My pulse rate spikes and I'm pacing the sidewalk, on the verge of crying. There's no reason for him to agree to lie for me. I'm not his girlfriend. We just recently became friends.

"Charlotte," he says softly. "What did you tell them?"

This isn't a harmless little white lie I'm going to ask him to tell. This is about murder. I should just apologize to him and tell the detectives the truth. "Wade . . ." I stare down at the sidewalk, at the cracks fractured through its surface and the weeds sprawling out.

"Charlotte," he says in an even softer voice. "I'm leaving school right now. Where are you?"

"I'm outside the police station. I should be home in about a half hour."

"Text me your address, and I'll meet you there. I'm not going to talk to the cops until after we talk."

"Thank you."

I text him my address as soon as we hang up, feeling a little more hopeful. Maybe Wade will understand why I lied and not get upset with me. Maybe he'll help me figure out what I should do.

On the drive back to Mr. Thatcher's office, he lectures me as if he's personally offended that I didn't tell him about the flat tire in advance. But all I want is to be left alone and for him to drop the subject, so I quickly apologize and tell him I just forgot to mention it. I'm not sure if he or Mom believes me. If I really had gotten a flat tire, I would have told Mom about it. I think she knows this.

CHAPTER 17

During the drive home with Mom, we talk about what happened with the detectives and Mr. Thatcher. She mentions how expensive it was to hire him. She had to pay a huge lump sum up front, with money she had to borrow. She's also concerned about her job security. The company she works for was sold recently, and the new owners have been downsizing. She doesn't want to give them any reason to let her go, so I assure her that I will be fine if she leaves to go on her work trip again.

Mom's hesitant at first, but she knows she doesn't have a choice. She has to go. If she were to lose her job, she wouldn't be able to pay Mr. Thatcher or our other bills.

As soon as Mom drops me off at the house, she heads back to the airport. I text Wade. He's just around the corner and shows up a few seconds later.

"Are you okay?" he asks, stepping into the house.

"I'm fine," I reply, even though I'm not.

Wade shows me the call log on his phone. "Those detectives called five times. Left two voicemails."

I immediately begin explaining -- in detail -- everything that happened the night of the party and everything that happened today with the detectives and Mr. Thatcher.

He cocks his head to the side and looks at me with his steely blue eyes. "Any guesses as to who stole your Bronco?"

I drop my gaze and notice his hand. Scabs dot the top of each knuckle, evidence of the fight he got into with the tattoo face. I rub the palms of my hands onto the thighs of my jeans and take a deep breath. The only enemy I can think of is dead. But clearly there's someone else out there who hates me enough to want to frame me for murder. "I don't know," I say. Tears begin to sting my eyes. "I feel so overwhelmed. I don't know who I can trust, except you of course."

Wade wraps his arms around me, pulling me in for a gentle hug. I melt into his chest, and the thrumming of his heart fills my ears. I'm not sure how long he holds me like this, or how long I've been crying. He doesn't push me away or let go until his phone rings.

"I better get this over with," he says, picking it up.

My body stiffens, and I'm on edge again, full of anxiety. He hasn't actually agreed to lie for me. I have no idea if that's what he's planning on doing.

Wade answers the phone. He agrees to meet with the detectives in a half an hour. As soon as he hangs up, he looks at me and nods. "I'll tell them we were together."

I exhale in relief, feeling like a weight has been lifted off my shoulders. But then the heaviness suddenly returns. A half hour is too soon. I feel like we need more time to prepare, like there's something I've forgotten to tell him. My entire future could very well come down to how the next few hours play out. Will Wade be able to convince the detectives we were together that night?

"So just to confirm what you already told them," he begins, "we met up at the party around four-thirty, decided to go get ice cream at Sonic and got a flat on the way back. You pulled over to the side of the road. I changed the tire, then we drove back to the party. Is that right?"

"Yes."

"What kind of ice cream did we eat?"

"Root beer floats?" I shrug.

"Okay."

I follow Wade to the door, amazed he is going to do this for me and at the same time still feeling guilty. "Thank you," I say, in all sincerity. My heart is so full of gratitude for him.

He turns back to look at me. "One more thing. When they ask me if we're seeing each other, what should I tell them?"

I'm caught off guard by his question, unsure how to respond. Us? Together? "You think they're going to ask that?"

"Of course they will." His beautiful eyes remain locked on mine, like they're searching deep into my soul. "I think we should say yes."

My stomach flutters. Is he joking? Wade still hasn't cracked a smile. I have no idea if he's being serious.

He places his hand on my shoulder, his touch electrifying. "Nevermind," he says softly. "I won't complicate things."

I stand at the door, frozen, watching him walk away. For some reason I feel like he's taking part of my heart with him. I might be making a huge mistake, or this might be the best decision I'll ever make. I can't believe I'm about to do this. "Wade," I call, running down the driveway. "Yes . . . we're together."

He stares down at me with his steely blue eyes. "Is that what you really want?" he asks in a gentle tone. I open my mouth to reply, and just then, he leans in and kisses me. Electricity shoots through me as his soft lips press against mine.

When we pull apart, he continues to hold me in his arms. "Are you sure?" he asks, his voice almost a whisper. I nod, because I'm unable to speak. And he kisses me again.

CHAPTER 18

To occupy my mind so I don't freak out over what might be going on at the police station with Wade, I open up my laptop and send friend and follow requests to all of his social media accounts. If we're going to be together -- as in boyfriend and girlfriend -- then we need to be connected in the virtual world too.

As I scroll through pictures on my Instagram account, I'm surprised and embarrassed at how many photos I have of Quentin. Why didn't I realize this before? What was I thinking? I'm bordering on stalker status here.

Moving at an urgent pace, I delete most of the photos, leaving only the ones of me and Quentin together with a group of people.

While I stare at my profile picture, I imagine what it will look like when I change it to a picture of me and Wade. Will we be holding hands? Hugging? Making silly faces?

Gemma's going to flip when she finds out about us. She'll want to know all the details, even the stuff she shouldn't ask me about -- the private, intimate stuff. But I guess there's not much to tell her about that anyway. Is Wade a good kisser? Most definitely. I can tell her that much at least.

I don't think Vivy will consider my new relationship to be that big of a deal. She doesn't seem to get excited about much in life. The closest she's ever come to smiling is a smirk.

I close my laptop, wondering if I'm jumping ahead or assuming too much about my new relationship status. Are things really that serious between me and Wade?

Sure, I told him I want to be together with him, and we

kissed which kind of sealed the deal, but is he really committed to me? What if he changes his mind? What if he realizes that I'm not *that great,* and he could do better? What if his idea of "going out" is a lot more casual than mine?

No, I've got to stop overthinking this. A new relationship should be an exciting and happy thing. I have a boyfriend. My first "official" boyfriend. He is handsome, fun, smart, brave. . . .

My mind lingers on just how brave Wade is. I wonder if he always takes risks. Is that part of who he is? Does he have any fear at all, or maybe he's just addicted to adrenaline? It might be the adrenaline. He rides a motorcycle. He's not intimidated by his older brother, Coop, who kind of scares me. He didn't back down from tattoo face. In fact, he went back for more. Maybe that's what I like about him -- his propensity towards danger.

I have dreamed about having a boyfriend forever, it seems. Only I never envisioned it happening under such crazy circumstances. If only there wasn't this underlying foundation of a murder investigation going on. What kind of a relationship can be built upon that?

Are we doomed for failure? How could our relationship ever amount to anything lasting and true when it's based on lies? I can't see us talking to our future kids one day about how we ended up together; how we snuck into a cemetery to open a casket half-buried in the ground, or how we lied to the cops because I had been accused of murder.

Leaving my computer behind, I get up from the couch and walk over to the refrigerator which is stocked full of Diet Coke. I grab a can and accidentally take too big of a swallow. The carbonation burns my throat, almost choking me. I set it down on the counter and scan the refrigerator shelves. I'm kind of hungry, but at the same time I'm too nervous to eat. I wish Wade would call.

I pick up my phone to check for messages, wondering how much longer he will be. What if they arrest him? What if they're coming here to get me next?

Honestly, I don't even know if I'm going to have another

day of freedom, let alone another week. Wade and I could end up being separated forever. Is that why I kissed him? Because I'm afraid our time is short?

I grab a second can of soda so I won't have to get up again and take it with me back to the couch. If I don't relax, I'm going to give myself an ulcer. There must be something I can watch on TV to distract me. I grab the remote and turn on an episode of The Great British Baking Show. The contestants are making petit fours. As I watch some of them fail miserably at making their dessert creation, I try not to think about Wade or worry about him, but I'm also failing miserably.

My entire future could depend on how well he convinces the detectives that we were together that night. Is he good at lying? I don't know. And even if he is a good liar, does this made-up flat tire story sound remotely logical or possible? I somehow just *magically* broke down on the side of the road, at almost the exact same spot where Bellany's dead body was found? Really? This sounds so dumb! I wish I could take it all back and come up with something better.

I turn off the TV and head to the kitchen again. Maybe baking something will calm my nerves. Chocolate chip cookies are Wade's favorite, so I decide that's what I'll make.

As I'm pulling out the last batch of cookies from the oven, my phone rings. I leave the oven wide open, drop the cookie sheet onto the counter and run to the coffee table for my phone.

Disappointment hits when I see the name on the screen. It's just Gemma. I don't know if I want to talk to her right now. Wade should be calling any minute. My phone continues to ring, but just before it goes to voicemail I decide to answer. "Hello?"

"Hey, Charlotte." Gemma's voice sounds tense, anxious. "So I just talked to Bridger. He said the cops brought you in for questioning today. Is that true?"

Bridger already knows? The detectives told him? Aren't they supposed to keep that confidential?

"So what happened? Are you okay?"

I tell Gemma an abridged version of the story I told the

detectives, including the part I made up about getting a flat tire and how Wade helped me change it. It's not easy to lie to her, but I don't have a choice. I've got to be consistent with my story and ignore the remorse and guilt I feel about deceiving everybody close to me.

Surprisingly, Gemma does not offer me any words of encouragement. Not once does she tell me that I shouldn't worry or that everything's going to be fine. I guess even my best friend can't deny my dire situation.

"So listen . . ." she pauses. "Because of all of this investigation stuff going on, I don't think it's a good idea for you to be around Bridger right now."

I sit down on the stool at the kitchen counter, preparing myself to hear Gemma relay to me Bridger's thoughts about all of this, which can't be good. She has already given me a big clue by telling me to stay away from him.

"You should give him some time. And space. A lot of space."

"What did he say to you?" I ask, afraid to hear the answer.

"Well, um . . . I think the cops have basically convinced him that you're the one responsible for Bellany's death."

The room feels like it's starting to spin. I lean onto the counter for support and close my eyes. How can I make this better? Is there anything I can do? "But my Bronco got a flat tire," I remind her. "That's the only reason I was parked near the woods. Do you think Bridger will listen to my side of the story if I call him?"

"I wouldn't do that if I were you."

"Why not?"

She sighs. "He's pretty furious right now, and I can't seem to talk any sense into him."

"But he doesn't know all the facts. I need to explain--"

"He knows all the facts," she cuts me off. "He and his dad talked to the detectives. Regardless of your reason for being parked on the side of the road that night, the fact is, you were at the scene of the crime, and that makes you look guilty." Her tone sounds condescending. I don't like it. What I really need is for her to be supportive and not judgemental.

I already regret making up that story. It was a huge mistake. All that did was confirm to the detectives that I was there. I should have listened to Mr. Thatcher and kept my mouth shut. But I cracked under the pressure. I let those detectives intimidate me.

"Charlotte?"

"Yeah," I mumble, not really interested in continuing this conversation.

"I'm concerned about you running into Bridger at school tomorrow," Gemma says. "Or anywhere else for that matter. Remember how he took a baseball bat to Terrence's car and how badly he damaged it? Sometimes I wonder what he would have done to Terrence if Bellany had been seriously injured in that car accident?"

I swallow hard. Is she serious? Is Bridger really that mad? "What did he say? Did he say he was going to hurt me?"

"Remember how crazy mad I got when Bellany ran over Whiskers? How I wanted to . . . you know--"

"*Kill her*," I finish her sentence. Bridger wouldn't be *that* angry with me, would he? Oh who am I kidding? Yes, he would. Bellany was his twin sister, and he adored her. "Did he say those words? Did he threaten to kill me?"

"Um, not those words *exactly*." Gemma doesn't sound convincing. I think she's lying. I think he did threaten to kill me. "Just stay home from school tomorrow, okay. Give him time to cool down."

Is school my only concern? "Am I going to be safe in my own house tonight?" I race to the front door and check the deadbolt to make sure it's locked. I continue to move around the house, checking all the windows and doors.

"He's not going to hunt you down." She chuckles, but it sounds forced. "You should just avoid him is all."

"Gemma, you've got to make him realize I'm innocent!"

"I know, I know! I am trying to do that. You know I

am. And I promise I'll keep trying. Just stay away from school tomorrow."

"Okay, fine."

As soon as we hang up another call comes through. It's Mom. She begins the conversation by asking me how I'm doing. The worry in her voice is palpable. She must feel guilty for leaving me.

I assure her I'm doing fine, because there's no point in telling her otherwise. It's not like she can do anything to make all my problems disappear. She's about to get on a plane to fly to Canada.

"There's something else I want to tell you," she says, voice strained. "Mr. Thatcher warned me that this might happen--it's merely procedural."

Procedural? "What's going on?"

"Since your Bronco seems to be a big piece of evidence in the detectives' eyes, he thinks they might want to inspect it."

"Are they going to take my Bronco?"

"It's possible. Mr. Thatcher said they could come by anytime to pick it up without warning."

My heart feels like it has stopped, and I need an electric shock to get it going again. The cops are going to comb through my Bronco, looking for traces of evidence -- evidence that could very well be there. The situation is worse than I thought. I know without a doubt, it's just a matter of time before they arrest me.

CHAPTER 19

I'm sitting in my Bronco, phone to my ear, still talking to Mom. I'm trying to assure her that I'll be fine if the cops do take my Bronco since I can ride the bus to school or get a ride with Gemma. I turn the key, and the Bronco's engine rumbles to life.

"Charlotte, where are you going?" Mom asks, alarmed.

"Just a quick trip to get a Diet Coke. And a chocolate bar. It won't take long." I don't tell her that I'm also heading to the car wash. I've got to hurry before it closes.

"Okay, well, don't be gone too long. Mr. Thatcher said it's very important that we cooperate with the police."

"Of course," I say to assure her. "This is going to be super quick."

Mom seems hesitant to get off the phone. I tell her repeatedly that I'll be okay and not to worry.

"I love you," she says for the third time and hopefully last.

"Love you too. Bye Mom."

The car wash attendant doesn't look pleased to work on my piece of junk Bronco, probably because I have purchased the most thorough and expensive wash they offer and my Bronco hasn't been cleaned in ages. I wait inside the building, feeling relieved I made it here before they closed.

My phone rings, and I'm afraid it's the police wanting to know where my car is. I look at the screen and see Wade's name. Finally! I already suspect things didn't go well with the detectives, otherwise why would the cops want to seize my Bronco? "Wade, where are you?"

"I'm still at the police station," he replies in a low voice.

"My mom's talking to the detectives right now."

Is that a good thing or bad? "I'm so sorry I dragged you into this mess."

"Hey," his voice is calm, but even lower now. "This is all just part of the game they play. They're trying to intimidate me." He sounds like he truly believes what he's saying, and he might be right. I certainly fell for their intimidation tactics. "I just wanted you to know so you don't worry. I shouldn't be here much longer. I'll text you when I'm done--gotta go." He hangs up abruptly.

I look out the window, watching my Bronco creep through the car wash, suds flying, scrubbers spinning. Breathe, I tell myself. Don't freak out. Stay calm. Wade is fine. He's not going to be arrested.

While I wait for my car to be finished, I start to form a plan in my mind about what to do next and decide that I need to focus all of my energy on finding out who stole my Bronco. If I can figure that out, then I'll discover who murdered Bellany.

After I tip the car wash attendant, I drive to the nearest fast food restaurant. I've already purchased a Hershey's chocolate bar from the vending machine at the car wash and I could have bought a soda there, but I don't want my soda in a can. I want a fountain soda with lots of crunchy ice. So I'm buying the biggest one they sell at Sonic. The Route 44.

Before I pull out onto the road, my phone dings with a new text message. It's from Wade. **I'm heading to work, running late. Everything is fine. Don't worry. I'll talk to you tomorrow and tell you all about it.**

Relief washes over me and at the same time I'm stunned. I can't believe he did it. I owe him my life.

I quickly type out a short response. **Thank you for everything! Can't wait to talk to you!** Since he's late for work, I decide not to tell him that my lawyer thinks the cops might want to seize my Bronco. I'll text him about it later.

I drive in the opposite direction of home, towards that cursed Highway two-ten in search of answers. On almost all of the detective shows I've watched, whenever they're trying to solve a murder, they return to the scene of the crime. That's what I'm going to do too.

As I approach the spot where my Bronco had been parked, according to the photo the detectives showed me, my pulse speeds up a notch. Darkness has fallen quickly. There aren't any street lights around here. Only the headlights on my Bronco illuminate the road in front of me.

I make a slight right turn at the bend in the road as a car pulls out in front of me. My nerves somehow get to me suddenly, and I change my mind. Instead of pulling off the road to park, I chicken out and continue driving. When I arrive at a stop light, I look over at the car next to me and my breath catches. Sitting behind the wheel is the rude blonde girl from the funeral. I wonder what she's up to.

She makes a right turn, but I'm unable to follow after her. Other cars have already pulled up and are blocking the lane, and there's a line forming behind me. I drive through the intersection, frustrated, knowing she'll be long gone by the time I get turned around.

At the next available spot I make a U-turn and head back down Highway two-ten, in an attempt to find the driveway the blonde had pulled out of. As I come to the bend in the road again, I spot a small red reflector, which I think might be the place.

I pull off the highway, onto a gravel road, where I'm immediately met by a no trespassing sign. My hands become sweaty, gripping onto the steering wheel. Tiny rocks grind under the Bronco's tires as I continue to drive down the path, deep into the woods. The narrow road is flanked by tall trees and sporadic deep ditches. If I wanted to get out of here in a hurry, I would have to shift into reverse and back up the entire way. But it's too dark to do that. I'm sure I would end up crashing.

Around the next curve, there's another sign nailed to a tree. I gulp when I read the words, *Trespassers will be shot!* Okay, that's it. I'm done with this.

I keep searching for a place to turn around, but the road

seems to be shrinking. Branches reach out and sweep across my Bronco. Eventually I see a light up ahead. It's coming from a small house. Four or five vehicles are scattered along the circle driveway in front of it. I'm about to flick my headlights off but stop when I see the road splinter up ahead. Yes! Finally a place to turn around.

I take the turn to the right, only to be disappointed. This road also leads to the circle driveway, right in front of the house. My foot hits the brakes, and I come to a stop beside a dilapidated shed, unsure what to do next. This shed seems big enough to conceal my Bronco. Maybe I should just leave it parked here and get out. My Bronco should be fine, right? I should be fine, right?

My hand rests on the door handle. The last time I wandered through these woods, Bellany happened. I cringe at the memory, at the bloody images that always seem to appear in my mind at the worst possible moments. I shake my head as if this action alone will erase it all, but it's useless. These memories are engraved in my mind, probably forever. I've got to push through this. I can't chicken out now. The cops are going to take my Bronco. I have to do this now. There is no alternative. I take a deep breath like I'm about to jump into deep water and push the door open.

Leaves and twigs crunch under my feet. I slowly close the door, trying to be as quiet as possible. Using my phone as a flashlight, I make my way towards the house while remaining under the cover of the trees. I pass by several disabled vehicles, some covered in weeds, others propped up on cinder blocks. There's an old waterlogged couch, a broken chair, a refrigerator with a missing freezer door, and several black trash bags piled up, contents spewing out.

The house has a blue tarp strewn across part of the roof. The windows by the front door are framed by crooked shutters. This can't be where that blonde girl lives, could it? She seems too put together, and she drives a nice car. I wouldn't think she'd live in a dump like this.

Music plays faintly, coming from somewhere inside the

house. I head straight to the backyard, passing by a boarded up window. There's more garbage back here, and a rickety old deck just waiting to give someone a splinter.

Mixed in with the music are several deep voices. These walls must be super thin, or the window is cracked open. I can hear almost everything they're saying. They're talking about someone's car, trying to diagnose the mechanical problem. A female voice enters the mix, and I instinctively recognize it as belonging to Vivy.

This must be her house. Wow. I bet she's embarrassed by its rundown condition. Maybe that's why she never invited me over. But, the blonde girl was just here.

At the party, Vivy acted like she didn't know her. Then they were together with Bridger at the graveside. Did they become friends somewhere in between those two times, or did they know each other before and Vivy was just lying to me?

I inch myself closer to the window, curious about who else might be in there with her. My fingers press against the moss-covered siding. I hold my breath, ready to fully commit and peek inside, hoping the darkness out here keeps me hidden.

My eyes widen, scanning the room. There's a fireplace with a fire burning, a tall shelf next to it. The TV sits opposite the couch where I can see the back of two men's heads. There's another guy sitting in a chair off to the side, a beer in his hand. Vivy's sitting on a lawn chair by the fire, staring down at her phone.

I duck back down below the window, unsure how much longer I should stay out here. The last thing I want to have happen is to get caught.

The voices in the room grow louder. And then I hear a new voice. It sounds familiar. A lump rises in my throat. Could it be? I inch up towards the window again. The beard, the tattooed arm, the voice -- it's Wade's stepbrother, Coop!

"What about me?" Vivy asks, turning to look at him. "Did you bring me anything?"

"You're the one who owes me. Like I told you before, you're

gonna be payin' off that debt for a long time." He jerks forward in his chair. "Did you just roll your eyes at me!"

"I-I was just looking at you," Vivy replies, a tinge of fear resonating through her voice.

"What are you doing here anyway? I told you I was hungry. Get in that kitchen and make me something to eat."

Laughter fills the air, and I crouch down again to hide.

"What do you want to eat?" Vivy asks.

"Make me some cookies. Chocolate chip. And don't burn 'em. If they don't taste right, I'm gonna make you do it again."

"But I don't think we have any eggs or chocolate chips."

"Then go to the store and get some!" Coop shouts. "Here . . . take this twenty. I want semi-sweet chocolate chips, none of that store brand cheap stuff. Real butter, not margarine. I'll know if you use the wrong stuff. And hurry up!"

"But I don't have a car?"

"Your brother will take you. Right, Dean," Coop says.

"Yeah, I'll take her."

I quickly leave the window and move around the house, keeping watch for Vivy and Dean. The front door slams. I wedge myself between the bushes, staying low.

"He thinks I'm his slave!" Vivy groans.

"It's your own fault," Dean replies. "Here, you drive. I've been drinking." He tosses her his keys.

"Isn't there something you can do to get Coop off my back?"

"Like what?" Dean snaps.

The truck door squeals as it opens. "I don't know. Do something to make him leave me alone."

"I don't think you understand the seriousness of the situation," his voice deepens as he climbs inside the truck, then slams the door shut.

"Yes, I do--" the other door slams. I can't hear what they're saying anymore.

The engine starts up, headlights turn on. I remain hidden in the bushes until the rumbling and the light fades. I wish I knew what they were talking about. What does Vivy owe Coop for? I don't want to assume the worst of her, but I can't ignore the implications of this mysterious debt she owes him. She's practically his slave, so it must be something huge.

Dean warned Vivy about the "seriousness of the situation." What did he mean by that? Did he mean *serious*, as in a matter of life and death . . . as in Bellany's death? Did Vivy murder Bellany, and did Coop find out? No. That can't be it. It couldn't be *that* serious.

Instead of walking around to the backyard again, I decide to leave. I don't want to risk getting caught by Coop or one of those other guys. And besides, it's getting late. The police might already be at my house waiting for me.

I ease the door of the Bronco shut then turn the key, cringing at the loud sound it makes, echoing into the still night. I shift into gear but instead of moving forward, the Bronco remains in place, tires spinning. Gravel rocks spray up, ricocheting off the metal, sounding like bullets. Crap! My foot stomps harder on the gas. The tires finally gain traction. The Bronco propels forward so fast, I'm unable to make the turn in time and change directions. I drive right past the front door of the house and speed off down the gravel road, hoping nobody saw me.

CHAPTER 20

The rapid speed of my heart rate doesn't taper back down until I'm driving along a busy road, about two miles away from Vivy's house.

I'm still in shock over how Coop treated her. It's like she is his personal little errand girl who has to obey his every whim. Why didn't her brother defend her? And where was her dad? She had mentioned that her parents divorced years ago, but other than that, I really don't know anything else about her home life.

As I turn down the road into my neighborhood, a sense of relief comes over me. I can see my house, and there isn't a cop car there waiting -- not yet anyway.

Our gray two-story home may not be fancy, but it's not an eyesore either. The windows are old and drafty, but they aren't broken or boarded up. There aren't any cars on cinder blocks parked out front or bags of trash bags strewn across the yard. There aren't any unwanted guests waiting for me inside like at Vivy's house. Mom rarely brings boyfriends home.

I leave my car key sitting on the driver's seat. Who knows if my useless attorney's prediction about the cops coming to take my Bronco will actually come true. If the cops don't take it, maybe someone else will steal it. Then my problem will be solved; no car means no evidence to convict me.

If the cops do end up seizing my Bronco, I'd rather it happen here and not while I'm at school. If it happened at school, that would be the absolute worst! I'd be the focal point of all the gossip, and I definitely don't need that. Just to be on the safe side, I'll leave my Bronco at home and find another way to school until the cops stop breathing down my neck, even if that takes months.

After I gather up my things, I take one last look around to make sure I'm not leaving anything behind. I look at the back seat and then the carpet on the floor. Should I try to clean it some more, I wonder. Would it even matter? There's really no way I would be able to get rid of all the microscopic pieces of evidence that might be in here. I would have to rip out the carpet and the seats. This is just a lost cause. I turn and head inside the house, feeling physically, mentally, and emotionally exhausted.

As soon as I slip out of my jeans and hoodie, I dive under the blankets into my bed, hoping to fall asleep quickly so I can escape all of my problems. By some miracle, I do manage to fall asleep.

When I open my eyes again, it's still dark outside. The clock reads 4 a.m. The exhaustion I had felt when I first got home is still with me, but I'm no longer able to sleep. My mind won't shut off. I'm thinking about Coop, wondering what he knows, and hoping Wade will be able to find that out. Is the rude blonde girl involved in some way too?

I climb out of bed, pad down the stairs, and immediately look out the window. My Bronco is still parked in the driveway. But I know it's just a matter of time before they come and get it.

There's an emptiness inside me, a feeling of despair, and it seems to be getting worse. What kind of justice exists in this world, if Bellany's murderer remains free, while I end up paying the price for something I didn't do?

Even though I'm not hungry, I go straight to the kitchen, fill a glass with milk and grab a handful of chocolate chip cookies. I end up eating five or six, maybe more. I don't know, I've lost count.

Since I'm already up and know I won't be able to go back to sleep, I decide to bake something. I open Grandmother's recipe book and start turning the pages until I come across her recipe for pumpkin muffins -- one of my favorites.

I open the fridge and pull out a carton of eggs. In the

pantry, I find the last can of pumpkin, then I search through the spices for the cinnamon. Once I gather up all the ingredients and have them set out on the counter, I take a look at the recipe again, making sure I haven't forgotten anything. Normally, I'm much faster than this and can remember everything I need without having to double-check, but my mind feels a bit frazzled with all that's going on. The words on the page blur for a moment. I rub my eyes and look again, now able to see clearly Grandma's handwriting.

When I was younger, Grandma and I used to go to bakeries and restaurants to taste their desserts. After she took a few bites, she would list off the ingredients she thought they had used to make the dessert, and I would write them down. Before we went home, we would stop at the store to buy the ingredients, then she would let me help her make the copycat recipe. Sometimes it took us several tries, but the finished result always ended up just as good or better than the original. I remember her saying to me that there was no secret recipe she couldn't crack, and she was right.

As the mixer hums, I take out a fresh sheet of paper and a pen. Grandma always wrote her recipes down, even the ones that she hadn't figured out yet. She said she could think clearer this way. So I figure I should follow her example and use this same method to come up with a suspect list. Hopefully I'll be able to solve this murder case, or at least figure out some more clues. I put pen to paper and start writing.

The rude blonde girl. Her motive for murder is unknown. She was flirting with Bridger at the party. Are they seeing each other?

During the funeral she cried. Was that because she felt remorse for something she had done to Bellany?

She secretly met with Vivy and Bridger at the cemetery. Was that just coincidental or were they scheming and plotting?

The rude blonde girl's alibi: she was at the party.

Gemma. Her motive for murder is hate and revenge. Bellany killed Gemma's cat, sabotaged her cheerleading tryouts, and ruined her chances with Bridger.

Gemma's alibi: she was at home on restriction.

Vivy. Her motive for murder is hate and revenge. Bellany gave Vivy the nickname, *Lice Girl*, which stuck with her all through middle school, essentially turning her into a social pariah. Vivy really didn't have lice but had a terrible case of dandruff.

Vivy is currently being blackmailed by Coop. Is that because Coop knows she's involved in Bellany's murder?

Also, Vivy met with Bridger and the rude blonde girl at the cemetery. She lied to me about being friends with the rude blonde.

Vivy's alibi: she was at the party.

Quentin. His motive for murder might be revenge. Maybe he found out Bellany was cheating on him with big G, so he killed her.

Quentin's alibi: he was at basketball practice.

Ruby. I can't believe I'm including Quentin's mom, but she did have a motive. Fear. She did not want her son to go out with Bellany, because Bellany demanded too much of his time. Ruby feared Bellany would ruin her son's future college prospects and his basketball career. Maybe she thought killing Bellany was the only way to get her out of her son's life. She has already murdered once before. What's to stop her from doing it again?

Ruby's alibi: unknown.

Ace. His motive might be jealousy or revenge. Could he be big G? Maybe he killed Bellany because she wouldn't break up with Quentin. Ace had scratches on his face the night of the party, possibly defensive wounds from Bellany's fingernails.

Ace's alibi: he was at the party.

Being at the party really isn't an alibi, though. With a house packed full of people, anyone could easily slip out of the house unnoticed, steal my Bronco, kill Bellany, then slip back into the party as if they had been there the entire time.

Quentin and Gemma are the only suspects who seem to have solid alibis. But what if they're lying?

I stare down at the sheet of paper, reading over my notes. How am I ever going to figure out which one of them did it? They all had a reason to kill Bellany.

I toss my pen aside. It rolls across the counter and lands on the floor. I give up! I can't do it. I can't figure this out. I pick up the sheet of paper, crush it in my hands, then throw it into the trash.

Even though I don't feel like baking anymore, I decide to finish making the pumpkin muffins so I can eat them. Who knows, I might end up having to endure eating prison food for the rest of my life. I better enjoy the good stuff while I still can.

By the time the first batch goes into the oven, I'm feeling a little more at ease. I'm not a trained detective, and I can't expect things to just fall into place. If the detectives can't even figure this out, then I shouldn't be so hard on myself.

I stand at the counter in front of Grandma's recipe book, and when I look up again, my eyes are drawn to the numbers on the oven timer as they count down. I close the recipe book and stare at the cover, remembering something Grandma used to say to me: "Trust your instincts."

Whenever she got stuck trying to figure out a recipe, she said she would listen to that little voice inside her head and it would tell her what to do. She said that's how she became such a great baker.

I close my eyes to clear my thoughts, focusing on my breathing, trying to relax. I continue to meditate until I'm interrupted by the timer going off. After I pull the muffins out of the oven and put the next batch in, I set the timer once again. Then I sit down on the kitchen stool, clearing my thoughts.

What are my instincts telling me? Anything? I pause and wait, but nothing comes to my mind. Lovely. My instincts are telling me absolutely nothing.

I open my eyes and watch the numbers on the digital timer tick down. This is stupid. All I'm doing is wasting time. Time . . . wait . . . that's it! I think my gut is telling me that I shouldn't sit back any longer and wait for things to happen. I have to make something happen and stop wasting time.

I was on the right track last night when I snooped around at Vivy's house. I didn't waste time. I did some actual investigating.

My plans for today are going to change. Originally, I was going to stay home from school and heed Gemma's warning to stay away from Bridger. But not anymore. I am going to school. I need to talk to as many people on my suspect list as possible. And I need to do it in person. Today. No more wasting time.

I think I should be able to avoid running into Bridger, if I'm careful. I'll just steer clear of all the places he typically hangs out, which shouldn't be that hard to do. I already know his class schedule.

Once the muffins are set out on the cooling rack, I race upstairs to get into the shower. While I'm blow drying my hair, my phone buzzes with a text message from Mom. She wants to know how I'm doing. Again. I send a reply right away so she won't worry, letting her know I'm fine and that the Bronco hasn't been picked up yet. Oh crap! How am I going to get to school? I look at the time and realize I've already missed the bus. I type out a text to Wade, explaining the situation. Luckily, he replies right away. He's coming to pick me up.

When I'm back downstairs in the kitchen, I set aside some cookies for him, placing them in a plastic container so they won't get smashed, then I wrap up a pumpkin muffin.

Standing in front of the bathroom mirror, I finish applying my mascara and a small amount of lipgloss. I wonder if Wade's going to be affectionate towards me at school in front of everybody. Will he hold my hand? Will he kiss me? Or is it too soon for stuff like that? Kissing in front of people at school is kind of a huge thing. Maybe we're not ready for that yet. No. Of course not. I shouldn't expect anything like that to happen.

When I hear the rumble of Wade's Charger out front, I grab my things and head outside. As soon as I slide into the leather passenger seat, my stomach flutters at the sight of his beautiful face, his tousled blond hair and mesmerizing blue eyes.

"Did you make those?" he asks, nodding at the cookies and

the muffin in my hand.

"I hope you're hungry." I set the cookie container down next to his phone.

He picks up the muffin. "What kind is this?" he asks, already unwrapping it.

"Pumpkin. Do you like pumpkin?"

A smile spreads across his face.

"I'll take that as a *yes*."

In between bites, Wade explains what happened yesterday with the detectives. "I stuck to the script just like we planned. And yes, they did ask me if you were my girlfriend," he says with a grin.

"What did you say?" I ask, returning the smile.

"I said . . . *yes!*" His voice grew louder when he said the word "yes," making me chuckle, and blush.

Wade takes a drink of his bottle of water, which I'm glad he has since I didn't bring anything for him to drink. "I think the detectives' strategy was to keep me at the station for as long as possible, in hopes I'd get nervous and contradict myself or say something incriminating."

"Those detectives definitely know what they're doing," I say. "I'm glad you didn't cave under the pressure like I did." The photo they had of my Bronco flashes through my mind. "I wish I had kept my mouth shut like my lawyer told me to. I'm sorry I dragged you into this."

A slight smile turns up the corners of his mouth.

"What?"

"My mom was afraid she'd have to post bail for me. She said she never thought I might end up being one of her clients."

My heart constricts. His mom must hate me. She probably told him I was bad news and to stay away from me. "What does your mom think about all of this?"

The Charger comes to a stop at a red light. Wade reaches over and tucks a strand of my hair behind my ear. The touch of his fingers brushing across my skin makes my stomach flutter. "Don't worry," he says softly. "She doesn't blame you." He looks at me with his alluring eyes, sounding sincere.

"If she ever found out that you're lying to cover for me, she'd absolutely hate me."

"Nobody's going to find out."

"But if this whole thing goes terribly wrong and we're looking at jail time, I'm going to tell the detectives the truth. I'll tell them you weren't there and that I made the whole thing up." I can feel my eyes stinging with tears. The thought of losing my freedom and Wade at the same time physically hurts. I hope that never happens.

A car behind us honks. The light has turned green. Wade focuses on the road again as the Charger accelerates. He takes my hand in his. "Everything's going to be all right," he says in his velvety smooth voice. "Girls like you end up living long and happy lives, with a loving husband and beautiful children. Trust me on this."

I know Wade can't predict how things will turn out for me, but for some reason hearing him talk about the future in a positive light brings me comfort, especially the part about having a loving husband and beautiful children. I wonder if he sees himself in my future.

As we continue the drive to school, I tell him about my conversation with Gemma and how she warned me to stay away from Bridger. Wade seems agitated to hear this. He's not smiling anymore.

I quickly move on to the next thing that involves his brother, filling him in on the details about what happened at Vivy's. "She has some kind of huge secret that Coop knows about, and he's using it against her. I wonder if it has something to do with Bellany."

"I'll talk to Coop and find out what's going on."

We arrive at school quicker than I expect. Wade opens my door for me and reaches for my hand. His touch makes me smile again. I'm amazed that I can feel happiness and excitement about our new relationship, even though I'm living a life full of turmoil. There's just something about Wade, though, and I can't quite figure it out. He has this ability to put me at ease. Maybe there's a special kind of energy radiating off of him that's impossible to see with the naked eye. Whatever this power is that he has, I'm definitely under his spell, and I don't have any natural immunity built up against it.

The parking lot is bustling with people. Several heads turn in our direction, watching us walk together, hand in hand. Soon after we're inside the building, Wade and I part ways and head to class. He doesn't kiss me, and I'm not sure if that's because of the school's policy prohibiting public displays of affection, or if it's for some other reason. Regardless, I'm kind of glad he didn't. People are already staring way too much.

I pick up my pace, hoping to get the opportunity to talk to Vivy and Ace before class starts. I'm not exactly sure what I'm going to say to them, but I hope I'll figure it out soon.

The classroom is mostly empty when I arrive. I'm relieved I have some more time to organize my thoughts. With my notebook lying open on my desk and a blank sheet of paper in front of me, I start writing down answers to the following question: What is the best strategy for getting information out of someone?

Is the answer intimidation, like the detectives did with me? Or what about bluffing? Should I make them think I know their secrets, when in reality I don't? Or how about manipulation? Should I try to make them feel sorry for me, so they'll have compassion and want to help? I guess that would only work if a person was capable of experiencing normal human emotions. Vivy seems to have a wall built up, barring anyone from entering her heart. This strategy probably won't work on her.

I sit and watch as people file in through the door, waiting anxiously for Vivy's bright red hair to appear, or Ace with his phone in hand recording his classmates.

My back stiffens when I see Ace walk in first. He pulls a set of headphones off his ears, and to my surprise he's walking straight towards me. "Sup," he says, taking a seat at the desk directly in front of me, which isn't his assigned seat. "I heard you got hauled into the police station." He shakes his head. "Those cops have gotta be nuts to think you had anything to do with Bellany's murder."

I'm stunned. What did he just say? He knows what happened? "How did you find that out?" I ask, keeping my voice low. "Who told you?"

His eyebrows knit together. "Bridger posted on Twitter. You didn't see it?"

I pull out my phone and scroll through Twitter but can't find anything from Bridger.

"Here," Ace says, handing me his phone.

I begin reading Bridger's posts, feeling sick to my stomach.

Charlotte Gray is a cold-blooded killer. #JusticeforBellany

Charlotte Gray's white Bronco spotted at the scene of the crime, according to numerous sources. #JusticeforBellany

Charlotte Gray, number one murder suspect according to detectives. #JusticeforBellany

The posts continue on, all with the same hashtag, Justice for Bellany. I can't read anymore. It's too upsetting. I hand Ace back his phone. Students continue to enter the classroom, staring at me like I've got a scarlet M for *murderer* sewn to my shirt.

"Listen," Ace says quietly, leaning in so close I can see the pores dotting the top of his nose. "I'm not going to jump on this bandwagon of haters at this school. I got your back. If there's anything you need." He thumps his chest with his fist. "I'll be there for you--*bam!* No questions asked."

Why is he on my side, I wonder. Does he really think I'm innocent? I guess it's possible. But why? Maybe he thinks I'm innocent, because he knows who the real murderer is. Maybe it's him. "Thanks," I mutter.

"Hang in there, girl." He winks at me as he gets up to walk to his desk.

How could I have not remembered the unyielding and

ever flowing river of gossip that exists at this school? Of course they all know I'm a suspect. I should have predicted this, prepared myself emotionally. A fellow student has been murdered and everyone's talking about it. There are reminders of Bellany all over social media and here at school: pictures, posters, flyers. I'm the one who helped Bridger put up all of the wanted posters around town. They're everywhere.

What I need to do is focus on what's important right now and set aside everything else. All of this gossip and all of the scorn-filled stares will end as soon as I find out who Bellany's real murderer is.

I look back down at the sheet of paper in front of me, moving my arm to uncover what I had written. I was supposed to question Ace and gather more information about his connection to Bellany. I guess I'll have to try again later.

My gaze shifts, and I notice that Ace had left behind a gum wrapper on the desk. I grab it and walk over to the trash can to throw it away. A cheerleader named Sandra Sanders is sitting nearby. She's watching me, staring at me. I try to ignore her, but she's being so obvious. I turn and look directly at her. "Got a problem?"

She rolls her eyes, flicks her long hair, but doesn't say anything.

I'm back at my desk again by the time Vivy arrives. Her backpack lands on the floor with a thud. She sits down in the seat across from mine, facing me. "How are you holding up?"

Maybe I will try the manipulation strategy. It's worth a shot. "As good as I possibly can," I grumble, "since everybody thinks I'm a murderer."

Vivy crosses her legs and props her chin on her hand, giving me her undivided attention. "Who would've thought queen B could still be causing so much drama?" She grimaces apologetically, but the look on her face seems more patronizing than empathetic. The bell rings and she turns to face the front of the room. Great. That conversation went absolutely nowhere.

As class begins, my thoughts linger on Vivy and her

connection to Coop. I'm not quite sure what I'm going to say to her after class. I can't tell her the truth; that I was snooping around her house last night, listening in on her conversation. I have to pretend like none of that happened, which makes confronting her a bit difficult. How do I get her to open up to me about her home life and about Coop?

My teacher is explaining the details of an upcoming homework assignment, but hardly anyone is listening to him. They're busy talking, and I think they're talking about me, because they keep turning to look. I'm probably the most hated girl at school now, which baffles my mind. I always thought that title would forever be bestowed upon Bellany. Except, most of the people who hated her, also idolized her. So it's not the same -- not even close.

In the parking lot earlier, I noticed people staring, but I thought they were just gawking at me and Wade since we're together now. A new couple is always gossip-worthy.

I sink down further into my chair. What if this animosity gets so bad, it affects my relationship with Wade? Does he like me enough to willingly endure all the scrutiny and hate he's going to receive because of me?

My teacher hands a stack of papers to the first person in each row to pass back. The girl in front of me lifts the papers up over her head and lets go of them before they touch my hand. The papers scatter in every direction, landing on the floor. I get up to retrieve them, anger building inside of me.

Bridger and his stupid Twitter rants! How could he turn on me so quickly? He's not going to give me the benefit of the doubt that I just might be innocent? I thought we were close, practically brother and sister. But I guess I was wrong.

When the bell finally rings and class is over, I stand next to Vivy's desk while she packs up her things. "Hey, can we talk for a sec?"

"Sure," she says, tossing her wavy red hair over her shoulder. The brightness of the red dye has faded, a lot. The color doesn't seem as jarring anymore. It almost looks natural now.

Her hazel eyes are lined catlike, and her lashes seem longer than usual. Is she wearing fake eyelashes? That's new.

As we walk out into the hall together, an idea surfaces in my mind. This just might work. "I was wondering if maybe we could hang out after school today?" I ask. "I could go over to your house."

"Can't," she replies without the slightest hesitation. "My dad sleeps during the day, because he works nights. I gotta keep the house quiet."

"How about later then, after he goes to work? My mom's out of town, so I don't have a curfew."

Vivy makes a face like she's about to rip off a bandaid from my arm. "I'm hanging out with Bridger tonight."

Suddenly a familiar and unpleasant feeling washes over me. I'm remembering how it used to feel when Bellany would swoop in and steal all my friends away back in middle school. Is Vivy choosing sides, and is she choosing Bridger's? "How about tomorrow?" I suggest.

Her gaze shifts over to the wall of lockers. People continue to pass us by like we're large rocks planted in the center of a stream, diverting the flow of water. "I made plans with Quentin. We're going to do homework."

My eyes travel down her outfit. I'm just now noticing that her pants are olive green, not black. It's a slight addition of color, but still, it's color. She scratches the side of her face, and I catch sight of her nailpolish, which isn't black either. It's blue. Vivy seems to be changing all of a sudden. What's going on with her? And why hasn't she offered to get together with me another time when she's not busy? Something's up. Maybe I should just confront her now. "How do you know Coop?"

"Who?" she asks, making a face like she didn't hear me.

Don't play dumb. "I know he was at your house last night. He said you owe him for something."

Her mouth suddenly gapes open. "How do you--where did you hear that?"

I step closer, staring into her deceptive eyes. "Coop is

Wade's brother, and in case you aren't aware, Wade and I are seeing each other now."

Her skin seems to turn a shade lighter as recognition enters her eyes. "They're brothers?"

"Yeah." I nod, crossing my arms.

"So what if I know Coop?" She shrugs, suddenly regaining her composure.

"He's blackmailing you."

She doesn't flinch, her expression remains hard. "Do you know how crazy you sound?" she asks in an even, measured tone. "He's not blackmailing me."

I ignore her insult, my focus firmly set on finding out any information I can. "What kind of dirt does he have on you? What do you owe him for?"

"Nothing. I don't owe him for anything."

"Yes, you do. I heard him say it."

She crosses her arms to match my posture. "Well, Coop's lying. I don't owe him for anything, Charlotte." Her eyes look me up and down. "Or should I call you Bellany? Because you're acting just like her."

I step in closer, holding her gaze. "If you're not going to tell me, then I guess I'll get the information straight from Coop. The only reason I asked you first, was so you'd get the chance to explain your side of the story before he does."

"He's not going to tell you anything, because there's nothing to tell," she says, chin lifted. "Congratulations, you've just become the new queen B." She steps around me and is swept up in the current of students making their way to class.

I'd rather be considered a queen B than a murderer any day -- I just don't want to be both. But whatever. I guess our friendship has sailed on now. It was probably going to be short-lived anyway.

At least I still have another option available to find out the truth. Coop. Hopefully Wade will be able to convince him to talk.

CHAPTER 21

The one minute warning bell goes off, which means I'm running late for my next class. From over my shoulder, I hear a group of girls talking about me.

"It's kind of hard to claim you're innocent when you're freaking car was there," a cheerleader named Jasmine Woods says. She's with three other girls. They're all wearing white ribbons in remembrance of Bellany, and they're all staring daggers at me.

I don't bother to respond or defend myself. They've already made up their mind and think I'm guilty. I let them pass, realizing that I should have gone down the other hallway. The classroom I'm standing next to is the one I originally intended on avoiding. It's Bridger's class.

My stride lengthens and I immediately speed up. Please don't look out here! When I'm in the clear, I still feel anxious and on edge. I round the corner at the end of the hall, and a jolt of adrenaline shoots through my entire body. Bridger's pacing back and forth outside my classroom.

I spin around, tennis shoes squeaking and race back around the corner, my eyes fixed on the girls restroom two doors away. Once I'm inside, I lean against the counter, heart thrumming rapidly against my rib cage. I don't think he saw me, but I'm still freaked out. I can't believe he was waiting for me. What was he planning on doing? Was he going to confront me and make a scene? I've never been on the receiving end of Bridger's wrath, but I have seen him dish it out to other people many times. He's gotten in several fights, and he's always the last one standing. But he wouldn't attack a girl, would he?

Gemma was right. I should have listened to her and stayed home today. There's no way I can avoid someone who is actively seeking me out. Bridger knows my class schedule, just like I know his. My instincts were wrong to come to school.

I retrieve my phone from my backpack, and my eyes narrow in confusion when I read what's on the screen. I have thirty-six new text messages. That's weird.

The first one is from mom, informing me that the cops have officially seized my Bronco. Good thing I didn't drive it to school today.

My finger quickly taps the next text message. It's from a phone number I don't recognize. Wait, all of these messages are from random, unfamiliar numbers. My stomach dips as I begin reading.

Murderer!!!

I hope you die!

You deserve to rot in jail!

There are more messages, but I already have a good idea what they say, so I stop reading. Someone has obviously taken the liberty of giving out my phone number. My guess is it was Bridger. Did he post it on Twitter or something?

I'm beyond ready to get away from all of these vicious people lurking around this school, and I don't think I can wait a single minute longer. I peek my head out the door and find Ace nearby, leaning over the drinking fountain. He stands upright and wipes his mouth with the back of his hand, noticing me. I motion for him to come. He willingly complies, with a big smile on his face as he enters the girl's restroom.

"What's up?" he asks, eyes scanning the stalls, probably looking to see if we're alone.

"I'm hiding from Bridger. He was waiting for me outside my classroom. Room 104."

Ace points over his shoulder. "I just walked by there and saw him." He hops up to sit on the counter, claps his hands together. "Tell me what's going on, girl. Did he threaten you? Do you want me to beat him up?" Ace raises his eyebrows. "Cause I will."

There's no way Ace could win a fight against Bridger -- a fact I'm sure he's aware of. Bridger outweighs him by fifty pounds and he works out. The only working out Ace does is with his fingers on his phone. "No," I shake my head. "I don't want you to fight him."

"So he threatened you?" Ace asks again, head bobbing side to side like he's upset for me.

"Not directly to my face. . . ."

"Well, that dude's still waiting there for you, so he must wanna do somethin'." Ace shakes his head. "That's just wrong. No boy should ever lay a hand on a girl. My momma taught me that a long time ago."

Since Ace's here, and I can't leave, I need to focus on the task at hand and pull myself together. It's time to start asking him some questions. "Do you miss Bellany?"

He cocks his head, feet stop swaying. "Miss her? I don't know."

I exhale, slouching my shoulders. Come on. Give me something better than that. "Were you close with her? I sometimes saw you two hanging out together."

He raises an eyebrow and nods, as if a new realization has just entered his mind. "Do you think she was my girl?"

"Was she?" I press.

"She was with Quentin. But you already knew that." He looks at me sideways, hand to his chest. "You think she was cheating on him . . . with me?"

"I don't know. It's possible."

"Quentin's my homie. I wouldn't do him like that."

"But she was so pretty."

Ace waves his hands emphatically. "Nah, I wouldn't do that to my boy."

I exhale in frustration. This is going nowhere.

Ace leans forward, holding my gaze and smiles. It's his smile that grabs most girls' attention. Yes, he's cute, and he knows it. "So you gonna ditch class and stay in here?" There's a certain tone in his voice, more seductive, suddenly serious.

I could tell him that inviting him in here was not an invitation to makeout with me, but I'm still hoping to ask him more questions, and I don't want him to leave yet. "Remember the night of Bellany's party, after the cops showed up?" I ask. "When I saw you with Stew, you had scratches on your face. It looked like someone had scratched your face with their fingernails."

"Yeah. I remember."

"Is that why you ran from the cops, because a girl did that to your face?"

"What? No." he replies, but he's not upset. He's still relaxed and very sure of himself. Overly confident like usual. "I fell when I jumped the fence. I already told you that. I never did anything to make a girl want to scratch me in the face. Girls love me. I'm harmless. Like a teddy bear." He bites his lip, suddenly seductive again. "How 'bout you and I get a little closer. We're all alone. Come on over here."

Okay. I think I've had enough of this. "I should probably get going," I say. "Could you do me a favor and check to see if Bridger's still out there? I just need a clear path to the exit at the end of the hall by the cafeteria, because I can't go out the front door by the attendance office."

He nods and smiles, both hands pointing at me. "How about I go with you? I don't have to stay at school."

Not a chance -- there's no way I want to be alone with him outside of school. I still think he could've been secretly seeing Bellany. Of course he's going to deny it. I just thought maybe I could get a sense of whether he was lying or not if I asked him, point blank. But I didn't pick up on any strange body language or nervousness that would suggest he was lying or hiding something. He may just be a smooth talker, an expert at deceit. He may be big G. And he may have murdered Bellany. "I don't think my boyfriend would appreciate me ditching school with you."

"You have a boyfriend? You're joking, right?"

Am I not girlfriend material? "I'm going out with Wade Toben."

He stares at me. "But I thought you liked mister hot shot basketball star, Quentin."

What? "Who told you that?"

His phone vibrates in his pocket, and he reaches for it. "I heard about your obsession with Quentin yesterday. . . ." he says as his fingers tap along the screen of his phone. "Your BFF, Gemma, told me."

Gemma? He's got to be joking. She wouldn't tell him that.

He points at me with his phone. "Gemma had just heard about the cops questioning you and wondered if they thought you murdered Bellany so you could have Quentin for yourself. You know, she thought it was your motive for murder." His fingers type on his phone again, eyes glued to the screen. "Every murderer's gotta have a motive. Unless they're nuts or it was an accident."

Anger flares inside me. Why would Gemma say such a thing, and to Ace of all people? Does she always talk about me behind my back?

Ace holds his hands up as if to surrender. "I didn't tell anyone." He sets his phone down on the counter, and yes I'm watching his phone like a hawk. I need to choose my words wisely, in case he's recording this conversation.

"Gemma's still your BFF." He shrugs. "She was just upset, and I happened to be there when she found out. She was really worried about you--thought you'd been arrested. She just needed someone to talk to. And hey . . . she made me promise not to tell anyone."

I don't care how upset Gemma was. She should never have confided in Ace. Never! I start pacing back and forth, trying to calm down. "Can you go check to see if Bridger's gone yet?"

Ace clicks his tongue. "Wade is slacking in his responsibilities. But that's okay. I don't mind being his stand-in."

A couple minutes go by, and I'm wondering if he got

busted for not having a hall pass.

The door finally cracks open, and I see his slicked back hair as he pokes his head in. "Okay, girl. You're safe now. He's long gone."

Our footsteps echo in the empty hallway as Ace accompanies me to the rear exit door. I'm about to walk outside when I realize there's a problem. I didn't drive to school today. Holy crap. How could I have forgotten?

Ace wedges his body in front of the open door to stop it from closing behind me. "You sure you don't want me to come with you?"

Ace has a car and could drive me home, but I would have to be crazy to go anywhere with him. I give him a look, which hopefully conveys the message to back off. He knows he shouldn't ask me again. I already told him no. "Not today." *Or ever.*

"All right then," he says in a sing-song way, as if I'm going to miss out. Pretty arrogant.

I cut through the parking lot, unsure what I should do or where I should go. There are some fast food restaurants within walking distance. Sonic is the closest. I could probably walk there in about ten minutes. I could order some lunch and hang out for a while. Then I could browse around the stores nearby until Wade gets done with school.

As I continue to weave through the vehicles in the student parking lot, I notice some movement. A car door slams shut, and a tall body appears. It's Quentin. We both freeze in place, eyes locked on each other. The meltdown he had at his house flashes through my mind. I'm remembering how he knocked over his chair, punched a hole in the wall, and destroyed his phone. But he doesn't seem very intimidating at the moment. He's not standing as tall as he usually does. He looks worn-down, troubled. The silence between us is beyond unbearable. Why doesn't he say something? Does he hate me too? Does he think I killed his girlfriend?

"I'm innocent," I blurt out. "Somebody is trying to frame

me." I wait for him to respond, scrutinizing his expression. Does he believe me?

Quentin continues to stare at me for a few more beats. "I know you're not a killer, and I also know what it feels like to be accused of being one."

I exhale, relieved and surprised. He actually seems more like his old self again.

"Who do you think is framing you?" he asks, sounding genuinely curious, bordering on concerned. But is this all an act?

Maybe you're framing me, or maybe your mom, I wish I could say. "I'm not sure."

He looks down at the ground, and when he looks up at me again, all I can see is distance in his eyes. This is the same way he looked at the cemetery. Physically we're standing close to each other, and yet he seems so far away. "Do you have an attorney?"

"Yeah."

"That's good. . . . I hope the police can find out who the real killer is, because this witch hunt it's getting out of hand."

"I know. Just because my Bronco was parked on the side of the road, doesn't mean I killed Bellany. I got a flat tire." For some reason, it's getting easier to lie about this.

He stuffs his hand in his jacket pocket and retrieves his phone. Is he checking the time? But he's already late for school. He needs to stay. I can't let him leave yet. "Did the detectives place you on the suspect list just because you were Bellany's boyfriend?"

"I think so." He frowns. "They hounded me with a bunch of stupid questions and wouldn't answer any of mine. Don't they think I want to find her killer just as much as they do?" The corners of his eyes wrinkle as his gaze shifts to something behind me. Am I about to get busted for ditching?

I turn around and see Wade walking towards us at a hurried pace, his tousled blond hair blowing in the breeze. Is something wrong?

CHAPTER 22

Wade palms his hair out of his eyes, slowing his pace as he approaches. "I just ran into Ace. I thought I'd give you a ride home."

"Yes, that'd be great. Thank you."

Quentin tosses his backpack over his shoulder, his attention solely on Wade, eyes not blinking. Judging by the stunned look on his face, I don't think he had heard the news about me and Wade yet. "I guess I'll see you around," he says, attention on me once again.

"Bye," I reply, attempting to tamp down my excitement over Wade being here. I don't want to rub our relationship in Quentin's face when he's grieving over the loss of Bellany. I just wish I knew whether his grief was because he missed her, or because he's sorry for killing her.

Before I climb into Wade's Charger, I cast a glance back towards the entrance of the school. Quenton's almost to the door now. I'm still kind of surprised he isn't mad at me, since I'm being accused of killing his girlfriend. Bridger absolutely hates my guts. Why is Quentin so forgiving?

"We better hurry," Wade says, prompting me to get in. "I don't want one of the security guards to stop us."

"Me either."

As we're driving down the road, the first thing I begin telling him about is my conversation with Vivy and how she denied knowing Coop.

"That settles it then," he replies. "Let's go talk to him."

We park a block away from Big Tony's Bail Bonds. The

neon open sign is lit up, but we don't go through the front door. I follow Wade around the side of the building into the alleyway. "My stepdad has security cameras out front and in the lobby. I don't want him to know I'm here." He picks up a rock and starts digging in the dirt, eventually pulling out a spare key.

"But isn't your stepdad inside working?"

"He doesn't usually show up until around three. But he keeps an eye on the cameras practically twenty-four, seven."

Once we're inside, we find Coop sitting behind a desk in one of the offices. The computer screen in front of him quickly goes black when he realizes he's not alone. His chair swivels around. "What are you two doing here? Don't you have school?"

"I need to ask you something," Wade says. "What kind of dirt do you have on Vivy?"

Wow. I'm surprised he just blurted it out like that.

Coop places his hands behind his head and leans back in his chair. "I don't know what you're talking about." His eyes travel over to me.

Wade waves his hand in front of Coop's face to draw his attention again. "What is going on with you and Vivy. We know you're blackmailing her. Tell us why. Does it have anything to do with Bellany Silverfield's murder?"

The chair squeals as he sits upright again. "Information like that isn't free."

Does he know something? My breath becomes shallow as anticipation swells inside me. Am I finally going to find out some answers?

Coop picks up a handful of darts from off his desk, shuffling them in his hands like a deck of cards. "One of you is gonna have to pay me. Otherwise, I'm not talking." He turns his chair, squaring his shoulders to the dartboard hanging on the wall at the far end of the room. He cocks his hand, then throws. The dart lands, missing the bullseye by a few inches.

"Forget it." Wade turns to me. "Come on. Let's go."

Seriously? We're just gonna give up? No. My feet remain firmly planted. I'm not ready to leave yet. "How much money do you want?" I ask, even though I probably only have around sixty dollars in my bank account, which is supposed to be for buying gas and food while Mom's gone.

Coop strokes his beard. "One-hundred thousand. That's the reward money they're offering." He chuckles. "Is that why you want to know? So you can get the money."

"Do you know who killed her?" I ask.

Another dart lands with a thud. "If I knew who killed that Bellany chick, don't you think I'd have collected by now?" He throws his last dart, then gets up to pull them off the board.

"Let's talk in private," Wade says to Coop, opening the door and walking out. Which I guess means I'm supposed to stay here.

Coop chuckles, setting down the darts. "Be right back, little lady."

I try to listen through the closed door, but their voices are muffled. What could Wade be saying to him, and why couldn't he say it in front of me? I pick up the darts and start throwing them while I wait. I hope Wade knows what he's doing. We can't leave here without getting that information. Somehow we've got to find out what's going on.

Eventually Wade and Coop walk back into the office. They're both silent. Coop takes a seat at his desk chair and faces me, sitting up straight all business-like. "Wade and I have come to an agreement. Among the terms, he has promised me sixty percent of the reward money, if you should collect." He raises an eyebrow. "Do you agree to these terms?"

Wade could have offered him the entire amount, for all I care. My freedom is worth much more. "Sure, fine."

Coop strokes his beard, thinking. "All right. I'll tell you what I know. But you also gotta agree to leave me out of this. My name is not to be mentioned to the cops. Got it?"

If only I knew exactly how involved Coop was, then I could make a more informed decision. I look over at Wade, unsure how to respond. He nods. "Fine. I'll keep your name out of this. Just tell us what you know."

"If you don't keep your word, there will be consequences," he says, pointing a dart at me.

Wade kicks the wheels on Coop's chair, making it wobble. "Knock it off!" his voice booms.

Coop gives him a defiant smile, picks up another dart and studies it, turning it over in his hand. "I'll tell you what happened. Nothing."

"What?" I ask, confused.

He shrugs, eyes landing on me. "Nothing. I've got nothing to tell you." A chuckle builds in his throat until he's laughing hysterically, buckled over in his chair.

I look at Wade, hoping for some kind of an explanation, but instead I see rage building on his face. This has been a total waste of our time. I don't know how Wade manages to put up with this idiot day after day -- no wonder he wants to move out of his house when he turns eighteen. I would want to get away from him, too.

"Come on," Wade says through gritted teeth. "Let's get out of here."

As I step through the office door, something crashes behind me, making me jump. Coop's laughter abruptly stops. I spin back around, expecting to see him and Wade fighting. They're standing a few feet apart from each other. Then I notice the dart board on the floor and the empty space on the wall where it used to hang. Did Wade just knock that down?

"Let's go," Wade says, his hand pressed against my back.

I'm expecting Coop to come charging at him any moment, even after we leave the building, so I walk quickly. Wade's jaw is still set tight when we arrive at his car. His entire body looks tense. "I'm sorry," he says in a strained voice.

"You don't have to apologize to me. I'm sorry you have to live with that guy."

He takes a deep breath and blows it out, palming his hair back. "You know what, I think we could both use some down time right now. Are you hungry?"

"Sure. I could eat."

"Where do you want to go?" he asks, pressing the button to start up the Charger.

"I don't care. I'd be fine if we went someplace for a hamburger and fries."

"I think we could do better than that," he says as the Charger accelerates, swerving around the car in front of us. "I know just the place."

We stop to eat lunch at a Mexican restaurant located close to downtown Smithfield. I've never been here before, and clearly I've been missing out. My chicken enchiladas are delicious. Wade's eating steak fajitas. I told him I don't want to talk about the investigation, Coop, Bellany, or anyone else. I want to take a break from all of that. He agrees.

Maybe I can count this as our first official date. And if, by some miracle, my innocence is proven and I don't go to jail, maybe Wade and I will end up staying together even after high school. Then one day when I reminisce about the past to friends and family, I'll tell them about eating here with him. But I'll probably leave out the part about us ditching school because I was trying to avoid the boy who thought I murdered his sister.

After we eat, we drive to a nearby park and sit there in his car, watching the geese float around in the pond. Wade tells me about his life before moving here to North Carolina. He grew up in Florida, lived there his entire life until he moved to Smithfield earlier this year. His biological father died from brain cancer when he was only five-years-old. His mom married his stepdad, Gilbert, a couple years ago. So most of his growing up was done without a father around.

"So what's the deal with you and Gilbert? Why doesn't he want you to work at his bail bonds business? Why is he kicking you out when you turn eighteen?"

Wade shakes his head at the thought and slouches down in his seat to get comfortable. "Coop stole money from his father and framed me for it. So now Gilbert doesn't trust me. And I don't want to cause problems for my mom, because she loves the guy. He treats her good and loves her. I figure the best thing for me to do is just be me, live my own life, make my own money and move out when I turn eighteen. One day Gilbert will realize that his son is more than an addict. He's also a lowlife, drug dealing, money stealing criminal." Wade shrugs. "I couldn't care less what he thinks of me. I know the truth and that's all that matters." Wade points at me. "What about you? Tell me about your family. I've heard you mention your mom before. Is your dad around?"

"My dad's not involved in my life." I pause and take a deep breath. Telling the story about my dad is never a pleasant experience. "I don't remember him at all. I was only two when he left. He and my mom moved every few months, because he kept quitting his job or he'd get fired. He had a hard time getting along with people, and he had a quick temper. One day his temper escalated and he hit my mom. So she kicked him out, changed the locks, put up security cameras, and got a restraining order. But that didn't keep him away."

"What happened?"

"I haven't told many people this. Gemma knows. So does Quentin." I pause and look out at the water, wondering how Wade will react when he hears this. "My dad came to the house one night while my mom and I were asleep. He started a fire, used gasoline as an accelerant. We barely got out of there before the whole place went up. My mom got burned on her back. I got burned on my stomach. But we survived."

The shocked look on Wade's face remains frozen the entire time I'm speaking. It's not easy for me to talk about this, but I want him to know about my past. I want him to know everything about my life. And at the same time, I have a hard time thinking about this man who could do something so terrible to the people he was supposed to love and protect. Was he just insane? Was he a sociopath? What was wrong with him? Sometimes I worry that maybe I might become like him one day, in some small way. I worry that maybe I have inherited whatever made him act out so violently and viciously, and this thought truly frightens me.

Wade's hand is on mine, and I didn't even notice till just now. "I'm sorry that happened to you. . . . Did he go to jail for what he did?"

I shake my head. "There wasn't any proof. But thankfully he took off and disappeared for some reason. My mom hasn't seen him, not once since then. We don't know where he lives or what he's doing. He could be dead for all we know."

"Did your mom ever remarry?"

I tell him about Mom dating Bellany and Bridger's dad. That was the longest relationship she's had since my biological father. "I used to want a stepfather and had hoped Mr. Silverfield would fill that role. What a mistake that was. But I didn't know their dad was nuts until after he and my mom dated. That's when I noticed how he would get mad at Bridger and Bellany for the smallest, most ridiculous things. One time he picked up the bowl of cereal Bridger was eating and dumped it over his head, because Bridger was chewing too loud. Another time, Bridger had made dinner and burned the garlic bread. His dad smacked him upside the head and tossed the rest of the meal, which was perfectly fine, into the sink and called him a screw up who can't do anything right."

"Did he treat Bellany that way, too?"

I didn't witness anything, not until I let it slip that Quentin's mom had a criminal record. I'll never forget that night. "I heard Mr. Silverfield slap Bellany. And I know he did something else to her that made her scream out in pain, but I wasn't in the room to see what he did. Mr. Silverfield is a terrible man."

Wade nods his understanding. "I guess when you spend enough time around a person, you eventually see their true colors."

My time with Wade ends before I want it to. He says he has to go to work, so he takes me back home to my empty house. I'm feeling more lonely than I usually do tonight.

My phone rings with a call from Mom. She's still worried about me. But I don't want to talk about the murder investigation, so I tell her about me and Wade.

"Your first boyfriend," she says, sounding more upbeat. "I can't wait to meet him."

"You're going to love him."

"Of course I will. He sounds really wonderful. . . ."

After we end our conversation, the decent mood I'm in quickly dissipates when I open up my Twitter feed. The first thing I come across is a hate-filled tweet, calling me a murderer. I quickly discover there are several more tweets just like it from people who I thought were my friends.

This has got to stop! I set down my phone and pull out my list of suspects from the trash can. As my eyes scan over the names, there's one name in particular that stands out to me for some reason. Quentin's mom, Ruby. I feel like I have got to talk to her as soon as possible. If she's innocent, then I'll cross her off my list. If I think she might be hiding something, I've got to bring this to the detectives' attention.

I send Quentin a text, asking if he wants to do homework together tonight at his house and explain that we can't do it at my house because Mom made me promise not to have boys over while she's gone. I also remind him about my nosey neighbor who will snitch on me. Quentin should believe the *no boys* rule. Mom sometimes insists on this, and the neighbor across the street has tattled on me before.

A couple minutes later a new message arrives. It's him! He needs my help with math, which happens to be my best subject. Perfect. Now all I have to do is talk to his mom while I'm there. What I'll say to her exactly, I'm not sure. Sometimes she can be so intense and intimidating, like she was at the funeral when she asked me who Bellany's enemies were. But bottom line, whether she's being friendly or not, I have to ask her where she was the night of Bellany's party. Does she have an alibi? Have the detectives questioned her? She should be on their suspect list.

Ruby had a motive: she wanted Bellany out of Quentin's life, because she thought Bellany was ruining Quentin's chances of being drafted into the NBA. If Ruby had found out that Bellany and Quentin were still seeing each other, I wouldn't put it past her to try to break them up for good. She obviously couldn't control Quentin by forbidding him from seeing Bellany. So what was left for her to do, other than direct her attention solely on Bellany? Ruby had to get rid of her, and she must have thought killing her was the only way to do it. Extreme? Sure. But not all that far-fetched -- not for Ruby, a woman who has killed before. She probably thought she would get away with it. And it sure looks like she might, if I don't do something to expose what she's done.

My stomach twists and turns, a bundle of nerves, as I wait for Quentin to come pick me up. I'm nervous about confronting Ruby, and I'm also nervous about seeing him. We're going to be alone together in his car. Is it going to be awkward? Is he going to act weird?

All I want is for things to be like they used to be. It was comfortable to hang out with him. And maybe it will be again. He kind of is already back to his old self, since he asked me to help him with his math homework. I wonder if he'll need my help with anything else.

Quentin usually has a hard time making decisions on his own, and unfortunately Bellany exploited this. Quentin used to dress like he was always on his way to basketball practice, wearing athletic clothing and tennis shoes. Bellany told him he looked ridiculous. She gave his entire wardrobe an overhaul, and he let her do it. Not only did she choose what clothes he wore, but she chose the music he listened to, the movies he watched, the food he ate. Yep, she even had him eating salads. No high school guy I know eats salads, not unless they're on a diet, and Quentin didn't need to lose any weight.

She always demanded his full attention, and time, nothing else was more important than her. Whenever Quentin had a test to study for or any other school commitments, she'd get all dramatic and accuse him of not caring enough about her. His grades suffered, because of her. If Quentin didn't return her texts and phone calls right away, she would accuse him of cheating on her. He used to spend hours and hours practicing basketball every day, until Bellany threatened him. She said, *Is basketball more important than me? If it is, then maybe I should find someone else to go out with.* He should have broken up with her right then. But he put up with her crazy ultimatums and mind games, basically letting her take control of his life.

When Ruby realized what was going on, she told Quentin to break up with Bellany. But Quentin didn't. He constantly lied to his mom. He'd tell her *I've got to go to basketball practice,* or *I've got to stay after school to get extra help with math,* when in reality he was going to see Bellany.

In the past, before Quentin started going out with Bellany, I was always roped into helping him, only I didn't take advantage of him. I didn't manipulate him. I just helped him choose between options, like when he picked out birthday presents for people, or when he chose which colleges to apply to. Why he asked me for help with all of these things, I don't know. It's not like I'm some guru who knows everything. Maybe he saw me as a sister, kind of like Bridger used to.

I didn't want to be thought of as a sister or even just a friend -- not with Quentin. I had wanted us to be more. I wanted him to choose me over Bellany. *Why didn't he choose me,* that question bothered me. Maybe the answer was that I never pursued him like Bellany did. But I wasn't as bold and confident as she was. I was too afraid of rejection.

I'll admit, I thought Quentin would see me as girlfriend material now that Bellany isn't around anymore. Yep, I was foolish and delusional. It's painful to recognize this in myself. I'm a lot more like Gemma than I realized.

But thankfully my feelings have changed now. I'm no longer interested in Quenton. My heart is *all in* for Wade. I think I'm in love with him.

Wouldn't it just be crazy if Quentin suddenly was interested in me? I wonder if it's at all possible. Hmm. Talk about the shoe being on the other foot. Strange. I never thought I would choose to relegate Quentin to the friend zone.

CHAPTER 23

The drive to Quentin's apartment goes smoothly, probably because I don't bring up Bellany or the investigation, and neither does he. This is my first time being back at his apartment since he flipped out and punched a hole in the wall. Surprisingly, the hole is gone now, and there's no indication that any damage was ever done.

The other thing that surprises me, is that Ruby has stayed in the family room watching TV the entire time I've been here. I keep expecting her to pop in and bring us a drink or a snack like she did before.

The anxiety inside me skyrockets when I realize that Quentin is working on his last math problem. Time is about to run out. Do it now, I tell myself. My hands push against the table as I scoot my chair back. "I'm going to go tell your mom goodbye."

Quentin's pencil stops moving and he looks up at me with his chocolate brown eyes. "She's not here. She's taking a yoga class tonight."

"What?" Panic rises inside me. I hadn't seen her car out front, but there were a bunch of cars in the parking lot. I thought maybe she had to park further away than she usually does. Is he sure she's not here? "But the TV is on."

"Yeah, I just forgot to turn it off."

"When will she be back?"

"She'll probably be gone until late. I think she said something about going out for a drink with her friends after yoga class."

No! I need to talk to her tonight. My Bronco is being inspected by crime scene investigators. If they find any of Bellany's DNA, they'll probably arrest me. I've got to find out who killed Bellany while there's still time.

Quentin sets his pencil down and closes his book. He stands and stretches, reaching his long arms overhead. "Ready to go?" Keys jingle as he pulls them out of his pocket.

I nod, gathering up my things. The disappointment inside me feels like it's literally crushing my chest, making it hard to breathe. This day is almost over, which means I'm another day closer to being arrested for murder. Why didn't I spend this time I had with Quentin more productively and ask him some more questions? He's still on the suspect list, isn't he?

"Do you want to hang out and watch a movie or something?" I ask.

"I've got to get to bed early. I've got a game tomorrow."

Crap. Not what I wanted to hear.

Quentin follows me outside into the moonlit night. The chill in the air gets to me right away, all the way to the bone. I quickly zip up my coat. The Camaro's heater blasts air through the vents, but it's not warm yet, so I reach over and turn it back down. Quentin seems to be driving a lot faster than usual for some reason.

My fingers squeeze tightly around my phone. I know what I have to do, the idea just popped into my head. How did I not think of this before? "So, Quentin . . ." I hesitate, unsure how to begin. "There's something I've been meaning to tell you. But I didn't want to bring it up, because I know this has been such a difficult time for you. I don't know if this is a mistake, what I'm about to tell you, but I think you should know the truth."

The Camaro slows back down to a normal speed. "What are you talking about?" he asks, giving me that same look he gave me when I showed up at his apartment after Bellany's funeral. Is he going to flip out? I guess it's possible, but I need to take the risk. I don't have the luxury of time.

I look down at my phone and unlock the screen. "I

recorded a conversation that Bellany had with someone she called, big G."

"A conversation with *who*?"

"Here. Just listen for yourself." I hit the play button and Bellany's high-pitched voice fills the air. Quentin listens intently, staring straight ahead at the road. I wonder if hearing this will bring him to tears.

When the recording finishes, we continue to drive in silence. I can't tell if there are tears forming in his eyes. It's too dark in here for me to see. Maybe I should apologize for springing this on him all of a sudden. "I'm sorry if that upset you," I say. He still doesn't respond. "Did you already know she was cheating on you?"

His head swivels and he looks at me for a few beats. The expression on his face is unreadable. Then he reaches up and wipes under his eye. Oh gosh. He is crying.

"You didn't know," I say.

He shakes his head and wipes another tear from his face.

"I'm so sorry, Quentin." I place my hand on his shoulder.

"I'm glad you told me," he says, his voice barely above a whisper.

My phone chimes with a text message from Wade. **Where are you?**

I'm with Quentin. He's driving me home. Why?

Don't go home! I just left your house. The cops are there waiting for you.

"What?" I gasp out loud, staring at the words on my phone.

Quentin glances over at me. "Something wrong?"

My heart is racing, and I'm feeling lightheaded. Why is this happening to me? "The cops are at my house! I can't go back there. Quentin, do not take me home!"

"Where do you want to go? Back to my apartment-- actually, no. They might look for you there."

I start typing Wade another text. **Can you meet us somewhere and come get me?**

Yes of course!

My finger taps the screen, ready to type another text, except I don't know what to write. I can't even think straight right now.

"What do you want to do?" Quentin asks.

"Wade is going to come pick me up. I just gotta figure out where."

"I know just the place. Tell him to meet us at the corner of Maple and Juniper, across from the abandoned gas station and that old bottling warehouse."

I quickly type out the directions and send it to Wade. A second later a new text arrives from him. **A cop just pulled me over, probably looking for you. I'll be there soon as I can.**

"The cops just pulled him over!"

"Really?"

"They're not going to arrest him, are they?"

Quentin palms his hair back, hesitating. "No. Of course not," he says, unconvincingly.

I'm in a constant state of panic the entire time we're driving. Quentin sticks to the backroads and side streets, so his vehicle won't be spotted by the cops. It takes fifteen minutes for us to get to the place we're supposed to meet Wade. Only I don't know if he's going to make it.

Quentin pulls over to the side of a deserted road next to a set of train tracks. He shifts the car into park, leaving the engine running so we can stay warm. His phone lights up with a call. "Hey, I've got to answer this. It's my mom. I'll be right outside." He gets out of the car, shuts the door, then starts walking down the road, phone to his ear.

My mind is a jumbled mess, full of incoherent thoughts. The cops must have discovered some of Bellany's DNA inside my Bronco. But how did they complete their search so quickly?

I clutch my phone in my hand, hoping Wade will text or call soon. What if he can't? What if they're arresting him right now, accusing him of being my accomplice? I guess it's up to me to prove that we're innocent. Somehow I have got to remain free and find out who really killed Bellany.

I wonder if the cops are looking for Quentin's car, hoping to find me. My only option might be to go on foot. As I consider everything I'll need to make a run for it, I notice that my phone battery is low. Crap! I would use Quentin's phone charger, but it's the wrong kind.

I open up the glove compartment, looking for another phone charger. As I shuffle through its contents, I find ketchup packets, napkins, a first aid kit, and a sandwich baggie with a bunch of little white things inside it. What are those? Pebbles? I hold it up to get a better look. What in the world? What's he doing with a baggie of teeth in his glove compartment? Are these Quentin's teeth from when he was a little child? Yuck! I toss the bag to the side and continue searching.

There's an old mobile phone in here, which I hope he'll let me borrow. Maybe it used to be his mom's. I pull it out and press the power button. Nothing happens. Great. The battery must be dead. I turn it over and study the pink case, noticing the small rhinestones. My stomach suddenly dips. Wait. I've seen this phone before. What in the world? This is Bellany's phone. Does he know this is in here?

No. He must not know. His mom probably left this stuff in here. Ruby borrows his car all the time. She must have driven it the night she . . . killed Bellany. I look at the baggie of teeth and want to vomit. Are those Bellany's teeth?

I can barely breathe -- I'm almost hyperventilating as I turn to look through the back window. Quentin's still talking on his phone. I grab a stack of papers out of the glove compartment and toss them onto the floor, wondering if I'll find more incriminating evidence.

My fingers continue to search frantically. Oh my gosh! There's something else! Mixed in with a handful of coins, I find a key attached to an Outer Banks keyring. A drop of cold sweat rolls down my spine. This is one of my lost Bronco keys. The driver's side door swings open. I jump and the key falls from my grasp. Quentin's silhouette hovers in the doorway as a train rumbles in the distance. Its whistle screams.

Quentin snatches hold of Bellany's phone. "What are you doing with this?"

"I found it in the glove compartment. Quentin, how did it get in there? Did your mom put it there? Did she kill Bellany?"

He carefully sets Bellany's phone down on the dash and stares at it like it's a bomb about to go off. Then he turns his head, looking at the key to my Bronco lying on the floor. "You shouldn't have been snooping around."

Judging by his reaction, this isn't the first time he has seen all this incriminating evidence. How long has he known that his mom murdered Bellany? Why hasn't he told anybody? "You knew all this stuff was in here?"

He doesn't move, doesn't blink. He barely looks like he's breathing. He has to turn his mom in to the cops. He's got to know this.

Finally he takes in a deep breath. "I don't want to have to do this, but you've given me no choice."

What is he talking about? What does he mean, *I have given him no choice*? I have nothing to do with all this stuff here. His mom is the one who murdered his girlfriend.

Quentin places his arm over the back of my seat and leans in, staring at me. His eyes look different under the haze of the street light. The warmth is gone. All I see is cold, and there's something else; something unsettling. I feel as though I'm looking into the eyes of a complete stranger.

I don't think he's going to turn his mother in to the cops. He's going to keep her secret. So what does that mean for me? What lengths will he go to in order to protect her? He wouldn't threaten me, would he? He wouldn't . . . try to hurt me, would he?

Quentin continues to sit there and stare at me with his cold, unfeeling eyes. He isn't the person I thought he was. I don't know him at all.

Somehow I've got to get away from him. I've got to do something. "Wade's gonna be here any minute," I warn him, my voice shaking.

"Are you sure about that? He is your accomplice, at least that's what you told the cops." Quentin swipes the screen of his phone and turns it so I can see. My breath catches. There's a picture of me from the night of the party. I'm in the woods, bent over Bellany's dead body.

"Where did you get that?"

"I sent this to the detectives earlier. Just like I sent that picture of your car." He lowers his phone and stuffs it into his pocket. "I'm going to collect the reward money when I turn you over to the police."

The reward money? How long has he been planning all of this? "If you turn me in, I'll tell them about all this stuff I found in your glove compartment."

He shakes his head. "They already have the photographic evidence, proving *you* killed her. And they're going to find Bellany's phone on *you!*"

This is insane! He can't possibly believe he can pin this all on me. "I guess it's your word against mine, then. We'll see who they believe."

"You're not going to say a single word to them about me. I won't let you."

"What? Stop talking crazy. What's wrong with you? You shouldn't be trying to protect your mother. This isn't worth ruining your life over."

His hand slams down on the dash. "My mom didn't kill her!"

She didn't kill Bellany? No! How could he? Quentin did it. He killed his own girlfriend!

What happened? Why did he do it? Did he find out she was cheating on him? Did he kill her in a fit of rage? Is he even sorry for doing it?

"Quentin," I swallow hard, "you killed Bellany? Why?"

"Shut up!" He jabs his finger into the air, inches away from my face. "The cops think you did it. Now I'm going to turn you in and get the reward money."

"But I'm innocent! And I know the truth! You're the one

who's responsible for her death. Not me! You're the one who's going to go to jail. Not me! What are you thinking? Have you lost your mind?"

He shakes his head, eyes narrowing. "The cops will think you did it. Because you're not going to be able to tell them anything about me; not when you can't speak; not when you're dead."

Dead? The word stings me. My whole body feels like ice is running through my veins. He can't be serious. He wouldn't do that. Would he?

"I know what you're thinking," he says, his voice ominous, devilish. "You're wondering how I'm going to do it. How am I going to kill you? Well, I'll tell you--"

"They don't give reward money to murderers!" I shout, cutting him off.

"Wrong again!" He leans in close, his hot breath on my face. "I'm not going to get blamed for your death, not when they rule it a suicide. You see, they're gonna think you killed yourself, because of the unbearable guilt you felt over murdering Bellany."

If he makes my death look like a suicide, then nobody will know the truth. Wade and I will get the blame for Bellany's murder. Wade will go to jail, and Mom . . . she'll be devastated. She'll have lost her only child.

Outside the car, the roar of an approaching train intensifies. This whole area is surrounded by abandoned buildings and endless vegetation. Wade's probably already in police custody, and nobody else knows where I am.

"You want to know how Bellany died?" Quentin asks, but I don't respond. I already saw her dead body. I don't need a play-by-play of what happened. I need to get out of here!

Quentin reaches in his pocket, produces a lighter and sets it on the dash. What's he going to do with that? He taps it with his finger, giving me a knowing look. "I burned her. Set her on fire."

That can't be true. Bellany was beat up and bloody. There were no burns on her. "You're lying!"

He grabs his phone and shows me another photo. My stomach churns. I swallow hard, fighting back the nausea building inside me. I avert my eyes from the photo of Bellany's charred remains and fold my arms over my stomach, over the scars that were left there by the fire my father had set. Quentin knows what happened to me when I was child. He's one of the few people I trusted enough to tell. If he did *that* to Bellany, what's to stop him from doing the same thing to me?

He cocks his head, staring at me with haunting eyes. "You know what it's like to get burned, don't you?"

My back presses against the car door. How could I have ever trusted him? How did I not see the monster inside of him?

A burst of light hits the back window. My fingers frantically feel along the door until metal touches my skin and I pull. I'm falling, twisting, gasping. My knees sting from the impact. *Get up!* The blaring train whistle pierces my ears, the roar of its engine builds, and the light continues to grow brighter all around me. It's so bright. I can't see. My feet stumble, legs push. I'm gasping for air as a single question continues to run through my mind: Am I going to die?

Something catches my foot and I fall. Pain surges through my knees and hands. I kick and punch, fighting to get away as he drags me along the ground. Rocks scrape and tear across the back of my legs. Suddenly his hands press down onto my shoulders. I can't move. Sharp, jagged edges needle the back of my head. A rod of thick steel runs directly under my back. No! He's holding me down on the train track! I'm screaming, but I can't hear my own voice. The train whistle is constant in my ears. I blindly claw at Quentin, trying to push him off of me as the engine roars, ground shakes.

Knees press down onto my arms, a heavy weight on my chest. My ribs and lungs feel paralyzed, unable to move or expand. I can't breathe. I need air! There's a pause in the shrieking of the train's whistle. Prickly whiskers press against the side of my face. Then I hear Quentin's voice boom in my ear. "I - am - big - G!" The meaning of his words barely register in my mind.

A sudden thud, and the weight on top of me is lifted. I suck in air, gasping for breath, scrambling to my feet. The silhouettes of two, maybe three bodies cut through the light. Wind whips through my hair as the train tears across the tracks in front of me. I can't see them anymore. I'm on the opposite side of the tracks!

I don't know how long I've been standing here, waiting for the train to finish passing, but it feels like an eternity has gone by. I still can't reconcile in my mind that Quentin just tried to kill me. The manner of death he chose was so . . . gruesome, violent, unthinkable! I can't believe he was going to hold me down and let that train run over me! How could he? I was his friend!

I take a deep breath in an attempt to calm my nerves but can't stop shaking.

When I was pinned down on my back, the train barreling down the tracks towards me, I didn't get a good look at the person or persons who tackled Quentin. Was it Wade? A cop? Whoever it was, if they had arrived just a few seconds later, I wouldn't be standing here right now. I would be. . . . No! I don't want to even think about what might have happened.

Whoever saved me, are they still fighting with Quentin? What if they got hurt? Or what if Quentin already won the fight? Hold on. What am I doing still standing here? Quentin might be waiting for me on the other side of this train. I need to get out of here!

With shaky legs I start to run, struggling to stay upright and not fall. Panting and out of breath, I slip in behind a thick tree trunk. The train whistle echoes in the distance. Darkness surrounds me. I check my pockets for my phone, but I can't find it. I must have left it in his car.

"Charlotte!" a deep voice shouts. "Charlotte, where are you?"

I turn around, peering through the break in the trees. A tall figure stands on the other side of the tracks, alone. Behind him, a single car sits parked on the street. I can't see the person's face. If it's Wade, then where is his car?

"Charlotte!" the voice calls again, finally coming through clearly.

My heart races. *It's Wade!* "I'm here!"

I run straight towards him until I collide into his chest.

"Are you okay?"

I bury my face in his neck and he holds me tight. No matter what happens, I don't think I'll ever stop loving him. Even if we part ways one day, I'll never be able to forget how I feel about him right now. "You saved my life!"

When we pull apart, he brushes his fingers across my cheek, wiping my tears. "Are you sure you're all right?" he asks.

Instead of answering, I kiss him. The feeling inside me intensifies, confirming what I already know. I'll love him forever. I almost say this to him when we pull apart, but I know I can't tell him. Not yet--not now! I'm about to lean in and kiss him again, but I stop when a terrorizing thought enters my mind. "Where's Quentin?"

Wade turns to gaze back at the street, and I realize the car parked there isn't Quentin's. It's Wade's Charger. My knees buckle a little. "Where's his Camaro?"

Wade palms his hair back, pushing it out of his face. "I don't know. He took off."

I swallow hard. "How long ago? Maybe we can still catch him?" I start towards his car, but Wade doesn't follow.

"He's long gone."

No! That can't be! "I need your phone?" I hold my hand out. "I need to call the police!"

"I already called. A patrol car should be arriving soon." He shakes his head. "You're not going to believe this . . ."

My gut continues to twist. More bad news? "What is it?"

Wade places a hand on the back of his head, wincing in pain. Sirens begin to sound in the distance. "Someone hit me in the back of the head with something hard, and I blacked out. When I regained consciousness, I saw another person sitting in the front passenger seat next to Quentin in his Camaro. . . ."

Wade pauses and shakes his head again.

"Who?" I gasp. "Was it his mom?"

"It was . . . Bellany. She's not dead."

My head starts to spin. I heard what Wade just said, but it's like the words are twisted, unable to register clearly in my mind. Blurry, flashing lights appear. Hands wrap around my waist to steady me.

In my mind, I can hear Quentin's last words once again: "I - am - big - G."

CHAPTER 24

Charlotte Gray
Journal Entry #1

One month has passed since Quentin and Bellany disappeared. The cops still haven't been able to locate them. Somewhere out there in the world, there's a six foot two basketball enthusiast, probably playing a pick-up game at some rec center or random neighborhood court. Bellany's probably sitting there watching him, with a different hair color to disguise her identity. The thought of the two of them roaming around as free people, together, makes me sick! Those two deserve to rot in jail!

I can't believe I didn't end up behind bars.

When Wade and I told the detectives what happened at the train tracks, I was worried they wouldn't believe us, and I don't think they did -- not at first. But we caught a huge break. I mean gigantic! The building across from the tracks where Quentin had parked, apparently wasn't abandoned after all. It had security cameras set up and was being used as a storage facility. Everything that happened that night was caught on video!

After further investigation, the police discovered that the burned body they originally thought belonged to Bellany, actually belonged to a teenage runaway from Virginia. They suspect that either Quentin or Bellany accidentally ran her over while driving under the influence. Quentin's Camaro had some body work done to it the day after the party, repairing the front bumper and right headlight. So now I know why Quentin didn't want me to check his car the night of the party. He didn't want me to see the damage.

The girl's burned remains served as a perfect substitute for Bellany's body since they were the same height. Bellany's abandoned Bronco was left on the side of the road about a mile away, near a traffic light, where it was sure to be noticed by the police. Some of Bellany's belongings were planted around the girl's charred remains. Otherwise, the investigators wouldn't have been able to identify the body. Fingerprinting was impossible, and the teeth had been removed, which explains why I found a sandwich baggie with teeth inside it, stashed in the Camaro's glove compartment. I still shiver just thinking about how I touched those.

Although I can't be sure, I suspect that I surprised Bellany and Quentin in the woods the night of the party. Quentin must have hid in the bushes, probably with the dead girl. Maybe Bellany panicked and decided to lay on the ground and act like she was dead. When Quentin saw me bent over her, he snapped a photo. I guess I mistook the flash of his camera for a set of headlights on the road.

The blood I saw on Bellany could have been her own, if she had gotten injured when they ran over the girl. Or the blood might have belonged to the girl and got transferred onto Bellany when they moved her body. But who really cares where the blood came from? All I know is that it was there. When I saw her that night, I didn't freak out over nothing. She looked like she was dead. Anybody would have thought the same thing as me.

As for Quentin's alibi, the detectives found out it was a big lie. Am I surprised? No. All he ever did was lie. He wasn't the person he pretended to be. He was an imposter. A monster.

The detectives discovered that Quentin was going to have basketball practice that night, but the coach had to cancel at the last minute. So his mom arranged for her boyfriend to vouch for Quentin's whereabouts, claiming he was the coach.

Big . . . G. I cringe just thinking about that stupid, idiotic nickname. I couldn't believe I didn't figure it out sooner! But it didn't dawn on me until about a week after the incident at the train tracks, how Bellany used to call Quentin a "big goober," whenever he annoyed her. The reason why I had never heard the name "big G" before was because she had just started calling him this name after her dad told her to break up with Quentin.

When I played the recording for Quentin of Bellany talking on the phone to big G, I truly thought he was broken-hearted and devastated. The tears, the sad expression, it all seemed so real. He totally fooled me!

When I think back to the night of the party, and how Quentin kept telling me that he was worried about Bellany, how he wondered if something bad had happened to her, I'm again amazed at what an expert liar he is. He had me convinced that he truly didn't know where she was. The entire time we were searching for Bellany, he knew she was perfectly fine! He also knew that I had seen her in the woods earlier and that I thought she was dead. My blood boils just thinking about this!

I still have unanswered questions. I'm unsure if it was Quentin's original plan to kill me and make my death look like a suicide, or if he made that decision when he saw me with Bellany's phone, the teeth, and my lost Bronco key. But he did drive me to the train tracks before I found those things, so maybe he had planned to kill me all along. Regardless, I have come to the conclusion that finding those things in the glove compartment, while it put my life in danger, it also saved me. If I hadn't found that evidence, I would have ended up spending a large chunk of my life behind bars for a crime I didn't commit.

As a side note, I found out why Coop was treating Vivy like garbage and ordering her around. She owed him money for drugs. Coop finally admitted this to Wade, after he learned about all the chaos Wade and I had been through with Quentin. I guess maybe he felt sorry for being a jerk. Oh, and the rude blonde girl is one of Coop's druggie friends.

Justice has not been served on Quentin and Bellany for killing that poor girl from Virginia. My heart goes out to her family and loved ones. Part of me wants to scour the entire world in search of Quentin and Bellany so they can face the consequences for what they have done. But the other part of me just wants to forget about everything.

No matter what happens with them, it is my goal and desire to live my life to the fullest. And I'm writing this down in my journal, so I won't forget: **I'm in control of my decisions in life, regardless of other people's actions.** From now on, I hope to always follow my heart, just like Grandma taught me. She taught Mom this same principle. And one day, I hope to teach it to my own daughter and granddaughter.

Here's another piece of silver lining under all of this madness: Wade and I are still together. I'm so grateful to have him in my life! His loyalty has already been tested beyond measure. I hope our future together will continue to be full of love, friendship, happiness and adventure, as long as the adventure doesn't involve murder.

CHAPTER 25

Bellany

Sometimes I feel like this pathetic world has been chewing on me for seventeen long years, grinding me between its teeth, and has only just now decided to spit me back out like a piece of inedible gristle on a steak. Maybe there's a parallel universe out there somewhere waiting for me, and I just got placed in this one by mistake.

It's painfully clear I don't belong here. I'm reminded of this as I stare at the back of the menu, catching its misspelled words: chicken fried **stake**, **tator** tots, fried **zuccini**. I memorized the entire menu within the first five minutes of working here, so I could give customers recommendations on what to order, because these idiots can't seem to decide for themselves. I'm surrounded by gullible, brainless, annoying people, who have no direction or ambition in life.

I realized that Quentin was just like most of these other fools in this diner when he said to me, "Let's just drive, Bellany. We can keep going until we run out of money." So that was his brilliant plan. He wanted us to wander around aimlessly until we had nothing left and nowhere to go, like a couple of mice in a maze with no cheese for a reward. When I heard him say this, I knew what I had to do. He basically made the decision for me with his foolishness.

"Order up," the cook calls from the back, drawing my attention.

I'm still standing here, waiting for this gray-haired, crusty old man sitting in the booth in front of me to make up his mind and order. Finally he lowers his menu, revealing his clouded glasses, which remind me of the murky sky outside. I hadn't seen the sun, not once since I arrived in the small town of Chehalis, Washington. The man's glasses slide down lower on his hooked nose. "Yes, the waffles do sound good. I'll have two."

I retrieve his menu with a smile, which is forced, but he doesn't realize this, because I know how to pour on the charm-- when I want to. But I hate acting like I'm happy, when I'm so mad at the world that I want to knock over, smash and break everything and anything I can get my hands on.

My fingers squeeze the handle of the coffee pot, much harder than necessary, as I fill his mug up. Then I walk back to the counter, taking the long way, in order to avoid passing by the police officer sitting at a table by the door, fork in one hand, knife in the other, sawing at a half-eaten pancake saturated in syrup.

I asked the other waitress to serve him for me, even though he's sitting at my assigned table, and I've only got one other customer. I made up an excuse as to why I couldn't serve him. I told her that he asked me out and I turned him down, but he keeps showing up here to flirt with me anyway, when in reality he has done nothing of the sort. The real reason I don't want to serve him is because I don't want him to recognize me.

I dyed my caramel-colored hair jet-black, and I wear green contacts to cover up my blue eyes. But I still worry it's not enough of a change. I considered cutting my hair but couldn't do it. There are some things that I just can't get rid of. I love my hair long. It's the part of me that still reminds me of who I used to be, Bellany Silverfield. But one thing I'll never forget, is what happened the night my life changed; the night I turned seventeen; the night I died.

My father had called that night, informing me once again, that I wasn't to see Quentin. Ever. If I did, he was going to send me away to boarding school until I graduated, then he would cut me off financially, totally disown me. He said that he would find out if I saw Quentin. He would ask Bridger. He would ask my friends. He would ask Bridger's friends. One way or another he would discover the truth.

So, I knew I had to be extra careful. I couldn't let anyone see me and Quentin together. We decided to meet in the woods where nobody else would see us. While I waited for Quentin to get there, I knocked back several beers. I was feeling a bit self-destructive. I was upset at my father for being so controlling and manipulative. It was my birthday and I had to sneak around to see my boyfriend. What kind of birthday is that?

While I was waiting for Quentin to show up, my dad called again. I almost didn't answer, but I knew that I had better or else he would accuse me of sneaking around with Quentin. Also, there was a small amount of hope inside me that maybe my dad's heart had softened; maybe he felt bad for yelling at me earlier and wanted to apologize and wish me a happy birthday.

How wrong was I? Well, the first words out of his mouth were, "Are you with Quentin?" Of course I said no. I actually wasn't with Quentin, not yet anyway.

Then he went on to tell me what a disappointment I had been. He told me that my mother called him crying, because I didn't answer when she called to wish me a happy birthday. I couldn't believe he was saying this to me. Of course I didn't answer when she called. I didn't want to speak to her. So I lied, hoping to diffuse his temper. "She never called me," I said. "She's just trying to get me into trouble, like she always used to."

My dad started yelling, telling me that he had never forgiven me for what I did to his wife (my mother). He blamed me for her insanity, which was totally ridiculous. He said that I drove her crazy with my mind games, my constant vicious insults, and my incessant manipulation. But it wasn't my fault that she was weak. He made her that way. I only called her the same names that he did: *fat, ugly, stupid, pathetic.* He was just as ashamed of her as I was.

Day after day, all my mom did was sit around the house in front of the TV. She'd eat and eat, and then she'd wash it all down with wine, beer, vodka, whatever she could get her hands on. My mother could've done something with her life, but she chose to be a fat, drunken slob with no ambition and no self-pride. What a wonderful role model.

One time she showed up at my school to bring me some lunch money, and she was slurring her words, talking way too loud, everybody in my class knew she was drunk, my teacher too. She was wearing this hideously tight outfit which only accentuated her bulging stomach and cottage cheese thunder thighs. This was one of the many times she humiliated me in front of my friends. I hated her for it.

My mom wasn't the only embarrassment in my life, though. Quentin soon became the other one. I can't believe I chose to place my entire future in his hands, but I kind of didn't have a choice. I was the one who was driving his car the night of my party. I was totally wasted when I ran over that girl. Quentin wanted to call the cops. He tried to give the girl CPR, but she was already dead.

I had to make him understand how serious the situation was, because he wasn't getting it. We couldn't call the police. I didn't want to go to jail. "We won't ever see each other again," I told him. "We'll be separated for who knows how long." I continued to paint the picture of a grim future for him, until he finally agreed to every single part of my plan.

At first, I just wanted to get rid of the girl's body so no one would know what happened, but when Charlotte showed up in the woods that night, I had to act fast. I was absolutely shocked to see her there. I thought she would still be locked in the basement, but somebody must have let her out. I knew if she caught me and Quentin with the dead girl, that would be it. We'd be going to jail for sure. I thought about killing Charlotte but doubted Quentin would agree. I had already pushed him far beyond what he was emotionally able to handle at the time.

I told Quentin to duck down and hide. "Wait until a car drives by with bright headlights, then take some pictures of me and Charlotte." I whispered this to him before I ran toward the clearing in the brush.

I dropped to the ground and laid there with my eyes

closed, hoping Quentin would take pictures like I asked him to. I heard Charlotte freaking out when she saw me. I knew she thought I was dead. There was blood all over my face from the accident. I had hit my head on the steering wheel. Quentin's classic Camaro didn't have airbags.

After Charlotte ran off, I got up and returned to Quentin so we could finish getting rid of the girl. Quentin was afraid Charlotte would call the cops or an ambulance. I gambled on the notion that she wouldn't. I knew that Charlotte would be afraid to tell anyone that she saw my dead body. She was such a coward. "No she won't," I insisted to Quentin. "She's too scared. Besides, she won't want to get blamed for murdering me."

He stood there stunned. "What do you mean, *blamed for murdering you*?"

Once again, I had to convince him this was the right thing to do. "When this dead girl's body is found, they'll think it's me. All I have to do is disappear."

"No! Let's bury the body so it won't be found."

"Do you have a shovel?" I snapped at him, tired of his stupidity. "All we have is this lighter. And after we burn her, we won't be able to get rid of her bones. We won't have enough time."

He paused, considering this, which only aggravated me more. We needed to hurry.

"I'll get rid of her bones," he insisted.

"No, you can't. You have got to get to the party so you'll have an alibi!"

Then I remembered something he had told me earlier. He said that he had found one of Charlotte's lost car keys. I immediately knew exactly what he should do. "Quentin. You've got to steal Charlotte's car. Drive it over to the spot where we hit the girl, park it there, leave the headlights on and take pictures of it. Make sure to take several pictures from different angles. Then drive it back to the party and pick up my car. Park my car at the intersection and then come and meet me here. I'll take care of the girl's body."

I think Quentin was in shock, because he really wasn't saying anything. He just nodded his head, staring off blankly, until I yelled at him. He finally snapped out of it.

The next night when he came to see me, I assured him once again that we would be fine, and we'd be together. Then I told him my plan about the money. "All you have to do is suggest to Bridger how helpful it would be to offer up some reward money. Trust me, Bridger will do anything to find the person who killed me. I know he will. Then Bridger will talk to my dad, and I know my dad will agree. He has a reputation to uphold in the community. He'll see this as another opportunity to show off all his wealth."

So while I stayed hidden in a hotel room, Quentin's one and only job was to frame Charlotte and collect the reward money, but he botched that up real good. He called me and told me that he had Charlotte in his car and that the cops were looking for her. I made him swear to me that he would turn her into the police. This was his chance to collect the reward money, just like we had planned.

But I sensed some hesitation in his voice. So I threatened to take off, told him he'd never see me again if he didn't go through with it. He had already messed up by bringing her to the train tracks near the hotel that I was staying at. But that wasn't the worst part. He then went on to inform me that Wade knew where they were. He said, "I didn't know what to do. Charlotte wanted Wade to save her, not me." What an idiot!

"What are you going to do when he shows up?" I asked, practically screaming at him over the phone.

"The cops will arrest him. He won't even make it here." Quentin's voice shuddered when he spoke. He didn't believe a word of what he just said.

I knew I would have to intervene. I left the hotel room and ran to where he said he was parked. I told him if he was still there when I got there, I was going to take matters into my own hands.

"What do you mean?" he asked.

"Charlotte is going to commit suicide tonight."

"No!" he shouted. "That wasn't part of the plan. We don't have to kill her."

"Fine, then you better tie her up to restrain her somehow and drive her over to the police station. 'Cause you know she's not going to go willingly."

But Quentin failed again, Charlotte took off, Wade showed up, so I had to hit him over the head with a rock to get him off of Quentin.

Thanks to Quentin's mistakes we never got the hundred thousand dollar reward, the cops know everything now, and they're looking for us.

Ever since that night at the train tracks, Quentin and I had been living off of his savings, which consisted of a measly three thousand dollars. We learned real quick that hiding from the cops isn't cheap, and we were down to our last five hundred dollars.

"So what are we going to do now?" I asked.

That's when Quentin had what he called a "brilliant idea." He wanted us to enroll in high school somewhere so he could play basketball and maybe still get a college scholarship. "We'll change our names," he said. "No one will know it's us. We'll be far away from North Carolina."

He was certain nobody would recognize him since he was wearing blue contact lenses and his hair was bleached blond. But his face and body still looked the same, a fact that I informed him of just in case he needed to be reminded.

How could he even think this was a good idea, let alone "brilliant?"

I told him his idea was probably the dumbest thing I had ever heard. But he wouldn't let it go. He kept bringing it up and no matter what I said to him, I couldn't change his mind.

He had the nerve to tell me that I was crushing his dreams. *Me?* I was crushing his dreams? What about what he had done? What about the money he could have gotten for us?

We started yelling at each other. I told him he wasn't good enough to play for the NBA, let alone get a college scholarship.

Things got out of hand. I slapped him in the face, and he pushed me to the ground so hard, I hit my head.

He didn't apologize. Nope. He picked up the stack of cash and said that he was going to do what he wanted to do with or without me. In that instant, I decided I had to get rid of him.

So I did.

The bell on the door rings, ripping me from my thoughts. Another customer has just walked in the diner.

"He's sitting at your table," the other waitress says.

"I know, Sloan."

Sloan leans back against the counter, a smirk on her pale, narrow face. She holds up a ten dollar bill between two bony fingers and flicks her head to move her fried, blonde hair out of her eyes, but a piece of it remains stuck in her silver hoop nose ring. "That cop just gave me this for a tip. And if you think I'm sharing with you, you're wrong, sweetie."

I hate it when she calls me sweetie. It makes me want to rip that crusty, disgusting hoop right out of her crooked nose. The last thing I want is a hand out from her. I've been more than patient with this girl over these past couple weeks since I first started working here. But I'm done now. She needs to learn to respect me.

"Darling," I reply, mimicking her syrupy sweet voice. "I don't want your money." My stare intensifies as I look directly into her eyes, shedding my nice and unassuming demeanor. "Get that out of my face or I'll jam it down your throat."

Her smirk disappears, and I watch as fear enters her bloodshot eyes. She looks away, chin lowered, and walks over to grab a plate of hot food for a customer, stuffing the money down the front of her shirt into her saggy bra.

From the corner of my eye, I see the cop rise to his feet. He's clean-cut, young, looks like he works out--only his upper body. He has puny legs and about twenty extra pounds on him. I could probably outrun him.

He continues to stand there, and I suspect he's looking at me, again, which is understandable. I tend to draw the eye of a lot of people, no matter what my color of hair is. I have a certain appeal that resonates with people who are looking for a certain companion, but not a relationship, I'm told. Even though I'm wearing this pathetic waitress uniform, this cop has noticed me. I caught him staring more than once.

I turn my back to him and start refilling the salt shaker. When I hear the bell on the door ring, I turn around and watch him through the windows as he heads to his police cruiser. Even though I'm clear across the United States, thousands of miles away from North Carolina, I know I still need to be careful.

The owner of the diner walks through the door next. It's forty-two degrees outside today, and he's sweating from the short walk he made from his car. Carrying all that extra weight makes almost every movement a struggle for him.

"Jessy, how are you today?" I ask with a smile as I pour him a cup of coffee.

"My back is killing me," he groans. "The pain pills my doc prescribed don't do nothing for the pain."

I set the hot mug down next to the register for him then retrieve a maple doughnut. "Have you tried CBD oil?" I ask. "I've heard it works wonders for people."

Jessy continues to complain about his pain while I finish preparing his usual breakfast order. Sloan is staring daggers at me from across the diner. I know she's jealous, because Jessy only ever wants to talk to me.

Jessy agreed to pay me in cash, off the books. I told him that I had left an abusive boyfriend and couldn't risk leaving a trail for him to track me down. I wasn't sure if Jessy would believe my story, or even consider breaking the law for me, but I figured it was worth a shot. So I poured on the charm, cried fake tears, and he bought it. Sometimes I'm able to manipulate people so easily, I surprise myself. Jessy had such compassion for me, that he introduced me to Veronica Crawly. She owns a hotel nearby, and she gave me a deal on a room. I clean a couple hours a day, and she lets me stay there rent free.

But I didn't decide to settle down here in Chehalis,

Washington for the free room and job at the diner. I decided to stay here, because I have a bigger prize in sight: Veronica's grandson, Roy. He's a senior in high school, eighteen-years-old, and he's going to inherit Veronica's estate, which includes several rental houses, the enormous home she lives in and the hotel.

Veronica's not in the best of health, so I don't expect her to live much longer. And Roy . . . sweet, trusting, kind Roy will serve as a good companion for me. We can enjoy his future fortune together, probably much sooner than he's anticipating, once I help Grandma along.

Maybe she'll pass away suddenly in her sleep from a heart attack. Maybe she'll die from tripping and falling down the stairs. Or maybe her death will be caused by carbon monoxide poisoning. I don't know. I haven't decided how it will happen yet. But she will die. Soon.

BOOKS BY THIS AUTHOR

They All Had A Secret: A Betrayal. A Deception. A Tragedy. A Murder. (They All Had A Reason. Book 2)

They All Had A Fear: A Past. A Debt. A Reckoning. A Murder. (They All Had A Reason. Book 3)

They All Had A Chance: A Pact. A Test. A Dilemma. A Murder. (They All Had A Reason. Book 4)

They All Had A Plan: A Passion. A Hatred. A Jealousy. A Murder. (They All Had A Reason. Book 5)

They All Had A Grudge: A Reason. A Secret. A Fear. A Murder. (They All Had A Reason. Book 6)

ACKNOWLEDGEMENT

As always, thank you to Denise. My cheerleader, advice giver, beta reader, my best friend.

To the Reader:
I hope you enjoyed this book and would love for you to leave a review/rating on Amazon! Thank you!

ABOUT THE AUTHOR

Michele Leathers

Michele Leathers was born and raised in sunny California with five siblings and now spends her days under the bright blue skies of North Carolina with her loving husband and three rambunctious dogs.

She received a Bachelor's degree in Philosophy from North Carolina State University. After raising a family, exploring multiple diverse career paths and at least as many different hair colors, she found a passion for writing.

Michele believes the most important components of a great story are interesting characters, loads of suspense, and compelling romance.

www.MicheleLeathers.com

Made in the USA
Las Vegas, NV
28 October 2024

d7b6409a-4a00-4610-8cc0-a9b177d7f306R01